I0835247

Roll Against Discovery

ALLYSON LINDT

ACELETTE PRESS

This book is a work of fiction.

While reference might be made to actual historical events or existing locations, the names, characters, places and incidents are either the product of the author's imagination or are used fictitiously, and any resemblance to actual persons, living or dead, business establishments, events, or locales is entirely coincidental.

Manufactured in the United States of America

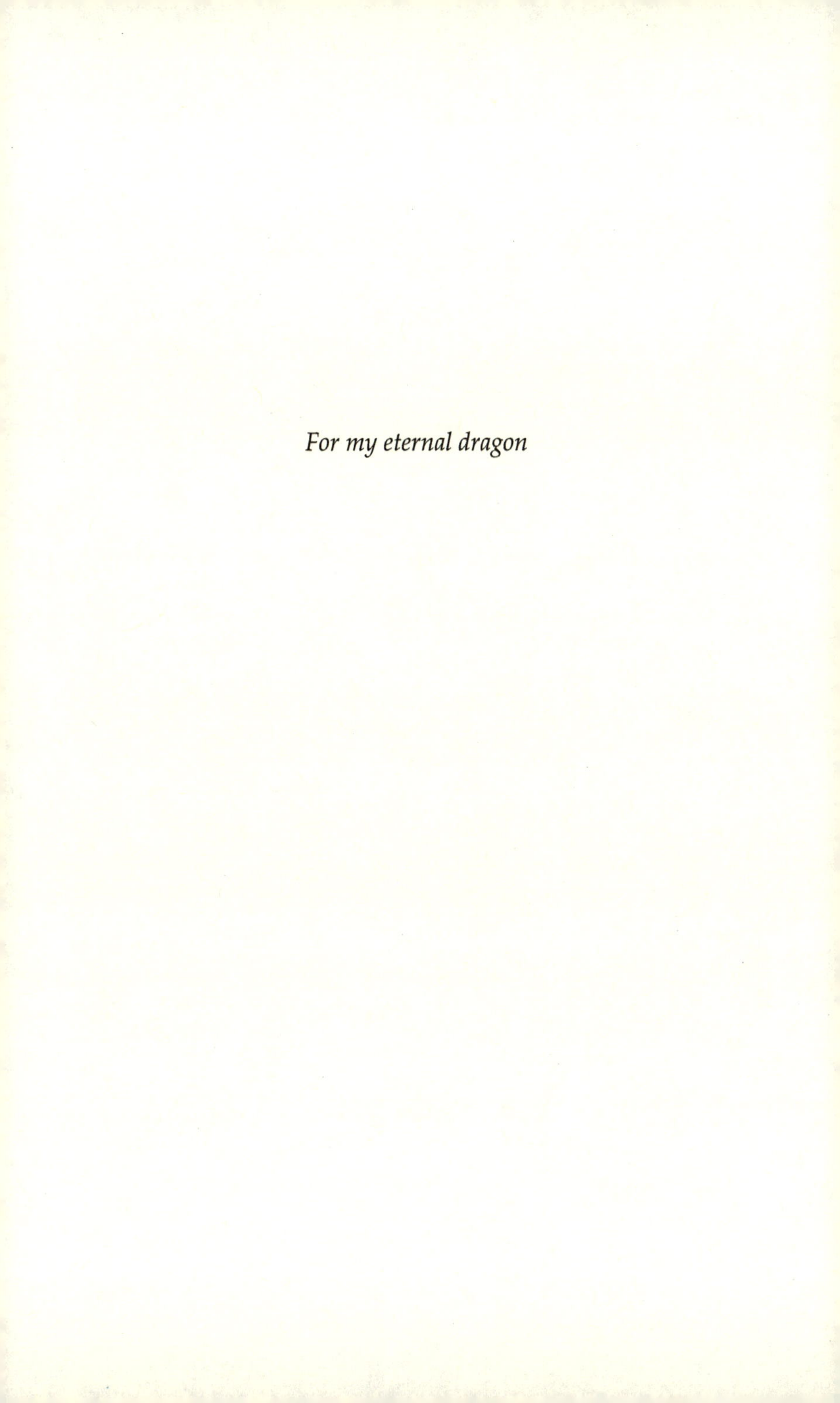

For my eternal dragon

When the elevator doors slid open, and I saw how many people were already packed into the car, I almost told them to go ahead without me. Someone dressed in a furry dog costume held the door, and another voice behind them said, "There's room for one more."

"I'm fine. I'll take the stairs." I waved the waiting people off with a smile.

"Come on." A friendly female voice joined in. "We'll make room." As if it were a command, a tiny path formed in the middle of the box.

Discomfort crawled through me at the seven or eight sets of eyes on me. Rather than drawing out the attention any longer, I stepped into the miniature crowd of costumed and casually dressed people. The throng closed back around me, assaulting me with heat, a dizzying array of perfumes, and early-stage body odor.

It might have made someone else wince and complain, but it drew my smile back out. This was one of the reasons I loved anime conventions, and also why I was staying in the hotel, even though home was only an hour away. The full immersive experience of fans who loved the medium as much as I did—or more—was intoxicating. Some of the guys at the call center where I worked gave me grief for being a twenty-five-year-old woman who spent her time watching cartoons. They had their fantasy football though, and I didn't see how this was any different.

If only I could get past my self-consciousness and let go, even for a few days, the way the people around me did... Then again, if I could let go of my insecurities, I might have gotten the job I wanted a few days ago, instead of being told I didn't have the personality it took to teach.

I ran my hands over my ass and down my thighs, to smooth out my costume. The skirt of my school uniform stopped halfway to my knees, so every time I moved, it felt like my white cotton panties were on display. I had a hunch I'd be reminding myself all day this wasn't the case.

If I were a bolder person, I'd have left the panties behind. An image nudged its way into my thoughts. I'd spill from the elevator with the crowds, wander into the hotel lobby, and catch the attention of some cute guy. He'd smirk as he looked me over, gaze lingering on my legs and chest. I'd pretend to drop something and bend at the waist to pick it up, giving him a private peep show. He'd introduce himself. I'd tell him I was Kathryn. Maybe we'd joke and flirt. He'd step into the elevator with me, on the ride back up. In the midst of the crowds, with people only paying attention to their own groups, he'd press close, slide a hand between my legs, and brush my bare mound.

The idea sent a naughty shiver through me, and I squeezed my legs together, to suppress the sudden pulse between them. Nope, as much as the fantasy turned me on, I wasn't that girl. I'd feel accomplished if I made it through the day without tugging my skirt down too often. My sensei at the Aikido dojo was probably right. Regardless of how skilled I was at the art, I didn't have what it took to stand in front of an entire class of people. All those eyes on me, those people expecting me to know what I was doing. The thought was almost enough to make me freeze.

We reached the lobby, and the pack around me dispersed. If I didn't stash the unpleasant memories of my missed job opportunity, I wouldn't be able to enjoy this weekend. I stepped aside, to keep from being underfoot, found a wall to lean against, and pulled out my program. What first? I wanted to visit the Dealers' Room and see what kind of neat trinkets I could lose my paycheck on, but it didn't open for another couple of hours.

"Captain." A male voice interrupted my browsing.

A second guy chimed in. "What are you doing

here alone, Captain? You should have an escort with you at all times."

I looked up from my program, to see two guys standing in front of me, both apparently talking to me. Or rather, to the character I was dressed as—the captain of a submarine, masquerading as a student. My pulse sped, as I traveled my gaze over them. Guy One had almost military-short brown hair and brown eyes I could fall into, and he filled out his T-shirt to the point I itched to trace the definition of his chest with my fingers. Guy Two was just as gorgeous. Spiked dark hair, pale skin, and green eyes. The contrast made my breath catch. He was a couple inches shorter than his friend, which still made him at least six inches taller than my five-foot-four. His shoulders were narrower, but that didn't stop my imagination from running rampant, planting either one of them in my daydream from a few minutes ago.

"I'm okay, really." My response squeaked out, and I cringed. I could have played along. Told them I'd love an escort. At least gotten in character long enough to ask their names. Why did I always think of these things too late?

Guy One quirked his lips in a half-question, half-smile. "Are you sure, Captain? We'd be happy to make sure your visit's enjoyable."

Yes. Yes. *Yes.* The simple but emphatic answer struggled against my shyness, but lost the battle. "Thanks, but I'm meeting friends real soon." It wasn't technically a lie. My brother, Jackson, and his partners would be joining me after they finished work that night.

"If you're sure," Guy Two—Mister Green-Eyes—said, "we'll take our leave." They both bowed from the waist, and Guy One gave me one last glance before the crowds swallowed them.

Regret pinged inside me, though it was better this way. They were cute to look at, but they'd be happier escorting one of the women who didn't mind squealing in joy and running up to random strangers for a hug who were dressed as their favorite character.

Now back to how to spend my morning.

I meandered toward the hotel conference rooms, keeping half an eye on my surroundings as I scanned the con schedule again. I could watch something in a viewing room, but I'd seen everything currently playing, and none of them ranked high enough on my list, to sit through again.

Laughter and chatter drifted from one of the rooms ahead. There was no sign to indicate what panel started next, but according to my schedule, it was an Alternate-Reality Game. The description read, *If you're looking for a game within a game, something to keep you busy and give you the inside track during your con downtime, check us out.* I paused in front of the door and glanced in. Unlike any other panel room, this had no chairs. Small groups of people milled about in front of a makeshift stage with a podium on it, chatting and laughing.

It looked like fun but also sounded like a lot of interacting with random people. I was about to move on, when my gaze landed on two people near the front. Guy One and Green-eyes from outside the elevator. Before I could think myself out of it, I let my feet carry me into the room, but I hovered near the back. There was no harm in checking things out. I tried to summon the courage to approach them. Someone else probably wouldn't hesitate. My heart hammered at the thought of walking up and casually introducing myself, and my palms grew clammy. Why couldn't I be someone else?

At least from back here, I could enjoy the view.

Someone stepped up to the podium. A woman, maybe a little older than me. It was hard to tell. A few other people turned to look at her, but for the most part everyone kept talking. "Let's get started, everyone." The woman spoke into the microphone. The talking continued. She turned to the man next to her and gave a slight shrug. He stuck his fingers between his lips, and seconds later, a shrill whistle threatened to split my eardrums. Silence washed over the room.

I massaged my ear until the ringing stopped. This ought to be interesting. Guy Two glanced behind him and met my gaze. My mouth went dry, and I licked my lips to try and get some of the moisture back. He winked before he turned back to the stage.

This was definitely going to be interesting.

2

"Better." The woman at the podium smiled. "Thank you, everyone, for coming. I'm Chloe, this is Jordan, and we're your contacts for the weekend. For those of you who've played these games before, let everyone who hasn't listen. The basic concept is simple—there will be a series of quests for you to complete. As you finish each one, it will lead you to a new task, and more of the story will unfold for you. Some goals and tasks will be obvious. Some not so much. Just because a clue led one person or group somewhere, don't expect it to do the same for you, as we'll adapt according to how you play. Recruiting new people—they have to tell us you referred them when they start—is worth bonus points, as are other things. There will be a grand-prize winner. The person who unravels the answer first. There will also be a bonus prize, for whoever gets the most bonus points.

"This isn't a purely altruistic gesture on our part; you're helping us test new software. The rules are simple. Sabotaging your fellow players won't be tolerated. You're welcome to work in groups or alone, though keep in mind more minds can give you different perspectives. And all the con's policies around harassment must be followed. Questions?"

The room erupted in chaos again, but one voice carried over it all. Guy One, with his seductive tenor. "That's all well and good, but it's really vague."

I nodded my agreement. I was familiar with the idea of an alternate-reality game. Basically, it was an interactive experience that used the real world and its participants as a medium. Role playing in tandem with reality. But it still didn't tell me much about what I should be doing specifically.

Chloe's smile grew. "It's supposed to be. If I give you all the details now, there's nothing left for you to do. Unless you've really twisted your head and viewed the situation upside down, very little of this will be what it appears on the surface. That being said, your first task is simple. Go out there, take cosplay pictures, and share them online using the hashtag RINARG. Where you post them is up to you, just make sure you've got the cosplayer's permission to post. Tag everyone in your group, including the cosplayer if they want, and it counts for all of you."

"That's it?" someone else asked.

Another voice chimed in "Boring.".

"Then don't play." Chloe stepped back from the podium. "It's up to you."

I let the idea roll over in my head. If the game wasn't what it appeared, what was it? Curiosity, both for the game and the attractive guys at the front of the room, spilled through me. A familiar voice nagged in the back of my mind. The first task involved talking to people to take their pictures, and odds were it would only get more social from there. I shoved the irritating voice aside. Screw insecurity. I took a deep breath, and summoned my courage past lingering uncertainty. This was a game, right? Why couldn't I be someone else for the weekend? There was no reason to be shy, withdrawn Kathryn, who didn't dare flirt back, let alone approach people on her own. I was going to dive into this and enjoy it.

My gut protested the decision, and I told it to hush. It was time to enjoy myself. Bold-me donned what I hoped was a playful grin, and strode toward the cute guys, who were fiddling with their phones. I swallowed my doubt and forced out my greeting. "Can I be your first model?"

Instead of replying, they exchanged a look I didn't know how to interpret. I'd expected a more enthusiastic response. So much for stepping outside my shell. I should leave now, before I made a bigger fool of myself.

Guy One turned a warm smile on me, his brown eyes almost melting my insides. "I don't know," he said. "It wouldn't feel right if we didn't even know your name."

Hope and giddiness sparked inside me, and I bit my bottom lip. I was bold. I was friendly. I didn't shirk. "Sounds fair to me, as long as it works both ways. I'm Kathryn."

Guy One shook my hand. "I'm Evan. He's Trevor." His grip was warm. Firm and tantalizing and enough to summon my earlier fantasy. Desire skittered over my skin. "I'm glad you changed your mind about us, Kitten. You did change your mind. Right?"

I seared the names in my mind, wanting to remember both for a long time. Kitten. The nickname rolled under my skin, and danced in my thoughts. "I'm still making up my mind"—I let the words roll past my lips without pause. —"but so far, I like what I see."

Trevor offered his hand next, and his touch was just as enticing. "I'm glad." He pointed his phone toward me. "Pose for me?"

Pose. What was I supposed to do? Panic flashed through me. I buried it under improvisation, set my feet at about shoulder width, bent slightly at the waist with one hand on my hip, and extended my other, fingers held up in a *V*. Any awkwardness I expected vanished behind the natural-feeling gesture.

They both snapped pictures and stood on either side of me, to show me the results. Trevor settled his arm against my back, and the sharp scent of cool body wash—probably with a name like Mountain

Spring—filled my head. His warm breath caressed my ear when he said, "Absolutely gorgeous."

Evan trailed a finger down my arm, drawing my focus. "Give me your user name. I'll tag you."

There was no way I was sandwiched between two hot men, both vying for my attention, and neither looking like he wanted to beat the crap out of the other. Maybe I was still asleep, dreaming soundly in my hotel bed. *If so, let it last a little longer.* I turned to Evan, my voice light. "I'll share, but only if you promise not to use it to stalk me."

He chuckled. "I prefer a much more direct approach than following someone in the shadows, who doesn't want to be followed. We like a woman who knows we're here, and who we know is interested."

My mind stumbled over the pronouns. He hadn't said *I.* I swallowed past a new lump of excitement. I wouldn't mind hooking up with either or both of them. Not that I'd ever done something like that before, but it sure sounded good in my head. No reason to get carried away, though. This was harmless flirting. An exchange of names and photos. It wasn't as if they'd invited me upstairs.

Then again, the day was still young. No reason to rule anything out. "I'm definitely interested." The words sounded awkward. Did people really talk like that? Neither of them was backing away from me in shock, so apparently it was the right answer. I gave them my user name, and seconds later received the alerts they'd both posted their photos.

"Hey, can we get a pic?" Someone new interrupted the conversation. I nodded and fell into my pose, for them and several more people. Ten minutes later, the crowd finally thinned, and then dissipated. I felt like my grin was permanent, and though my cheeks ached, the quick burst of attention had been a blast.

Happiness fluttered through me that Evan and Trevor still waited, just out of range of all the cameras.

"You're practically famous now." Evan dragged his gaze over me, leaving a path of heat in its wake. "Can we say we knew you way back when?"

"I have a better question." Trevor held up his phone, as if to take another picture. "Will you still volunteer to be our model if the next challenge involves a fan service shot?"

Fan service, in short, was a term for showing a hint of something provocative. My pulse stuttered, and then raced ahead at a full gallop, with bold-Kathryn at the reins. "Are you asking to see my panties?" I forced my voice to sound coy. At least I hoped it did.

"He's asking"—Evan stepped closer, voice low and gravelly—"to take a picture of you flashing your panties." Unlike Trevor's scent, his was a faint musk.

My bravado faltered. "Not in public." Crap. That's not what flirty, fun Kathryn should say. It wasn't that I didn't like the idea. On the contrary, the suggestion filled my head with all sorts of delicious images. The kinds of things normally relegated for alone-time with my vibrator. Putting on a private show for the camera. Knowing the guy on the other side was turned on by the teasing. My nipples tightened at the idea, straining against the satin of my bra. "I mean, that's the kind of thing that's better done discreetly.

"We have a room," Evan said. "If you wanted to take us upstairs, you should have just asked."

There was that plural again. *Us.* The notion they knew exactly what they were doing filled me with a new level of trepidation and excitement. "You started it," I said.

"It's true"—Evan turned me toward the door—"but we'd rather not finish it alone."

"We're still talking about the pictures, right?"

"For now." Trevor stepped next to me.

Hesitation raced back in. Being bold was one thing, but I'd known these guys for less than half an hour. And *known* was a generous term. I wanted to say *fuck it* and go along with them, but I couldn't silence my concerns enough to make that leap. "Who decides if it's about more?" I tried to keep my tone light, but a shadow crept in.

Evan shifted enough to look me in the eye. "You have the final say. I promise."

He seemed sincere. They both did. But could I trust my gut on this? "I just..." I wanted to give a clever answer. Something to keep the conversation going, instead of scaring them off. Words failed me.

The idea was enticing, but I couldn't find a way past my doubts.

Evan studied me for a moment. "You said you were meeting people later. Right?"

"Yes."

"Text one of them. Give them our room number. Tell them to send management up if they don't hear from you in an hour." He paused and furrowed his brow. "Unless you're not interested."

The ache of my nipples hard and straining against my bra insisted I was, and my curiosity and sense of rebellion wanted a reason to say *yes*. I hesitated a moment longer, before sending Jackson a quick text. Then I turned my smile back on the guys and let the fun glide back into my response. "Behave, or someone comes knocking when our time is up."

Evan intertwined his fingers with mine, and Trevor placed a hand at the small of my back, both of them prompting me toward the elevator.

"I never promised we'd behave. Just that we wouldn't misbehave unless you wanted to," Evan said.

My heart hammered in my throat, and damp excitement grew between my thighs. I had no idea how I got myself into this, but I was going to enjoy it for all it was worth.

As we stepped into their hotel room, anticipation spiraled through my veins, but my newfound confidence evaporated. It was easy enough to fall into the joking and flirting when I didn't have time to stop and think, but I stood in the middle of a room, with two gorgeous men who seemed very interested in me, and I had no idea what to do next.

Evan placed a finger under my chin and forced my gaze to meet his. "Are you all right?" His voice still held a seductive tone, but it was laced with concern. Staring into the deep pools of brown that were his eyes sent a sense of comfort over me, but it wasn't enough to bring my thoughts back under control.

I nodded. Damn it, where had my voice gone? "I'm good. Great even."

"May I?"

I wasn't sure what he was asking. That didn't stop me from saying, "Yes."

"The thing is"—Evan settled his hands on my hips, gaze never leaving mine, and turned me so I stood between the two of them, back to Trevor and his camera—"it's all about the teasing and seduction." He glided his hands down my hips, toward the edge of my skirt. "Not about being obvious." He jerked his arms, and I turned my head in time to catch a glimpse of my skirt flipping up. Cool air brushed the back of my legs, and the camera flashed.

Excitement returned in a rush, bringing my smirk with it. "I think I see what you're saying."

"Show me." Trevor's command dragged icy heat down my spine.

I twisted so he faced my side, and pulled up my skirt, hand on my hip. He continued to snap shots, as I twisted and turned. A tiny voice in my head told me I looked ridiculous. I banished the doubt it insinuated. I hooked my thumbs in the elastic of my panties and tugged the waist down enough to expose skin.

Evan stepped behind me and covered my hands with his, halting me mid-pose. I caught my breath and leaned back into him. "Careful, Kitten." His chest vibrated against my back with each word. "Do you really want to take things to that level?"

Yes. My brain screamed with the answer. I wanted to hear him say it though. There were some assumptions I wasn't willing to make. "Depends on what that involves." My voice came out husky.

He nudged our hands and my clothing a smidge lower. "It probably starts with me stripping these out of the way. Are you willing to bare it all for the camera?"

A fresh wave of arousal spilled through me. I had to be soaked by now. "Only if we all enjoy it."

"Trust me, we will." Trevor pulled up a chair and dropped into it, viewfinder still pointed in our direction.

"Then yes." My agreement tasted wicked.

Evan dragged down my panties, leaving a trail of delicious friction behind. I stepped out, and he tossed the clothing aside. Still behind me, he flipped the front of my dress.

Trevor snapped another picture. "You shave." His appreciative gaze lingered below my waist. "You get hotter every minute."

"Wax," I said. Stubble drove me batty.

Evan stepped in front of me and looked me over. "God, I'd worship a pussy that gorgeous."

Was this a good idea? The lust spilling through me insisted yes, but habits and the fact this was all being captured on camera gave me pause.

Fuck it. If I was going to be someone else for a few days, I'd go all out. The moment for hesitation was gone. I was going to live this moment, whatever happened, and not let my inhibitions stop me. I dropped onto the edge of the bed, knees together. Enjoying the feeling of two pairs of eyes watching my every move, I trailed my fingers up my thighs, spreading my legs with each passing inch, until I had exposed myself again. "I like the sound of that."

He shook his head with a throaty chuckle. "You do realize the kind of worshiping I want to do is hands-on?"

I'd hoped, but the acknowledgment called to the need pulsing from my sex. God, was I really putting on this show for two complete strangers? And inviting one to participate? Even my dreams weren't this vivid. Apparently, my imagination needed to step up its game. The entire arrangement felt surreal, but I'd never been more turned on. From my rigid nipples to my swollen clit, my entire body ached for attention. I opened my legs another inch and glided my finger over my smooth, slick lower lips. I gasped at my own light touch and the moisture that coated my fingertips. "I definitely like the sound of that. Show me."

Trevor kept the camera trained on us. The outside attention heightened every nerve in my body. Evan knelt at my feet and kissed up the inside of my thigh. The scuff of stubble on my sensitive skin coerced a groan from me. I whimpered and squirmed when his hot breath caressed my wet mound, but instead of making contact, he kissed a path down my other leg. I was intensely aware of the clicks of the camera phone with each new shot. The fact Trevor still took pictures spiked my arousal.

Evan dragged his thumb up my slit. "You're so wet, and I've barely touched you. Showing off is a turn on?"

A bigger one than I'd thought possible. Every inch of me hummed like a live wire, singing with each new caress. "Only for the right audience."

"In that case, lucky us." He blew on my wet skin, and a pleasant shudder rolled over me. Seconds later, his tongue followed the path his thumb had drawn. When he wrapped his lips around my tender button, a moan tore from my throat. I leaned back, supporting my weight on my wrists, and closed my eyes. He traced dizzying patterns with his tongue, and my groans grew louder and more punctuated. He lingered on the area, sometimes pressing harder, then pulling back when I ground against his face. The teasing buildup already had me on edge, and the wax and wane of contact drew my climax closer to the surface.

"Fuck," Trevor muttered. I heard the distinct sound of a zipper sliding down.

Was he…? The notion he might be jerking off to the show made my head spin. Evan shoved two fingers inside me without warning, and sucked harder on my clit. Orgasm built inside, spilling through my veins, rolling over me, consuming me as I cried out. I pressed against Evan until his touch became too much, and then I pulled him up and crushed my mouth to his. The taste of musk and sex —of me—lingered on his lips.

He tangled his fingers in my hair and yanked. Shock surged inside, filling me with a need for more. Of him. Of this. Of all of it. He forced his tongue in my mouth, and it danced with mine. A frantic dance for dominance. A drive to be closer.

He pulled back with a ragged gasp, held my head, and looked me in the eye. "Though you may not believe this"—a gravelly current undercut his words — "we really did only want pictures. But Christ, you're hot. I need to be inside you."

I nodded over his shoulder. "You're sure Trevor doesn't mind watching?" I didn't have a problem with it.

Evan kissed up my neck, a series of hard sucks and hungry nibbles, until he reached my earlobe. He caught the flesh between his teeth and tugged lightly, before letting go. "I'm sure he'd rather join in."

His words rumbled over my skin, and my brain jolted to a stop. It wasn't as though the idea of multiple partners was a foreign one. Jackson was in a poly relationship. Except that was the big difference—he was committed to his partners. Besides, I was boring, shy Kathryn. This wasn't the kind of opportunity that presented itself to me. Except apparently, it was. The idea of being with two guys at once, the fact it was about to become more than a fantasy, brought back my arousal full force.

"Are you okay with that?" Evan asked.

Logically, reasonably, in everyday life, I shouldn't be. I couldn't talk myself out of wanting it though. The entire idea made my body hum for more. "Absolutely."

It didn't take us long to shed our clothes. I wasn't sure which sight I appreciated more. Trevor's wiry frame and pale skin, with cords of muscle trailing through his forearms and a trail of dark hair running from his navel downward, or Evan's defined chest, six-pack abs, and—oh, my hell—those lats. One of them had condoms. I wasn't even sure who.

Evan sat on the edge of the bed and tugged me toward him. He laid a trail of kisses along my hips, over my stomach, and up my chest. Each feather-light touch tingled through me, culminating in a sharp need between my legs. My clit throbbed, wet and eager. I'd never been interested in continuing after I got off. Not by myself or with one of the few boyfriends I'd had. Right now, seeing them get off—and me at the same time—was an all-consuming thought.

Two fingers slid between my pussy lips from behind. Trevor. I groaned. He nipped at the soft skin where my shoulder met my neck, and stroked between my thighs. He pressed close, his chest meeting my back, and his groans rumbled through me.

Evan lay back on the bed and tugged me forward. "I want to watch you ride me. See your face this time, when you come."

I straddled him. He covered my hand and directed it back to wrap around his cock. He grunted when I grasped his thick shaft. Trevor continued to stroke me, spreading my juices to my ass. I guided Evan toward my opening, pumping him slowly, rhythmically. Hovering above the head of his dick. My senses chirped and jumped in anticipation. Each new touch was another switch on my arousal. When Evan thrust his hips up, driving himself inside me and spreading me open wider than I ever had been, I cried out. The delicious burn spread through me, swelling and growing as he pumped.

Trevor shifted his attention toward my ass, slipping easily along my slit. A finger nudged my second opening, and a new shock of pleasure filled me when he pushed in.

Evan cupped my ass and squeezed so hard I was sure he'd leave a mark. The idea heightened my excitement. He glided his palms up my spine, pulling me toward him until my chest pressed into his. Crushing my hard nipples against his skin. Each time he slammed inside me, he hit a tender spot that made my lungs squeeze for air and my toes clench. "Have you ever been fucked in the ass before?" he asked, holding my gaze captive.

I'd never even been asked so bluntly before, but I still had enough sense to remember I was playing a part. Beyond that thought, the rest of me was lost in the new and incredible touches. I forced myself to nod. "Of course." My reply came out a dry rasp, and I licked my lips.

He raised his eyebrows, but if he doubted my answer, he didn't say so. He moved his palms back to my butt cheeks, gripping and spreading.

Trevor's finger slid out of me, but I barely had time to process the shift in sensations before something much larger nudged my back door.

"Relax." Evan slowed his rhythm.

I tried, but my first reaction was to clench against the intrusion. I forced myself to breathe, and when Trevor began entering me, I thought my head might burst in a shower of sparks and pleasure. He dug his fingers into my hips and inched in, rocking in time with Evan. The slow push in took a few moments, and stretched me in ways I'd couldn't have imagined, filling me up, pressing into new areas and flaring with bliss. His hips met my ass, and I knew he was buried inside.

The pace increased again, quickly becoming frantic. I didn't know where to focus. The sensations were all new, intense, and overwhelming. Evan cupped one of my breasts, and squeezed hard, in time with the pounding. He pinched the nipple. Rolled it between his fingers. Tweaked enough it hurt. Climax rolled through me again, building in my belly, merging with the delicious pain in my chest, and culminating between my legs, until my orgasm ripped a shout from my lungs. I lost myself in the moment, riding the waves as they crashed over and through me.

The feeling didn't ebb the way I expected. It receded for a moment, and then rushed back, full force. I heard a grunt or two. The men slammed harder against my frame, more punctuated. Fingers gripped my hips harder, Trevor's short nails digging into my flesh. Evan shuddered underneath me in a series of gasps and groans, before slowing.

The room spun. Or maybe it was the lack of oxygen and blood in my brain. I struggled to catch my breath, and clung to the edge of enjoyment bursting through me. Trevor slid out of me first, and I reluctantly rolled off Evan to collapse between them on the comforter.

The three of us lay sprawled in the middle of the king sized mattress. They looked as dazed as I felt. Evan tangled his fingers with mine, and Trevor rested his head on my thigh. The sounds of breathing returning to normal and the occasional happy sigh mingled with the climate control. My mind was numb. I liked that.

A mechanical whistle shrilled through the air. My heart leapt, trying to jump through my ribs, and the two bodies next to me jerked. I laughed and pressed one hand to my chest, feeling the pulse hammer against my palm. I reluctantly extracted my fingers from Evan's, to reach for my phone. "Sorry."

Trevor squeezed my leg. "At least your friends are looking out for you."

Sure enough, the message was from Jackson. *You okay?*

Had we really been up here for an hour? Wow. I sent back a quick, *I'm good, thanks.* >.> <.<. The emoticons at the end would let him know it was me sending the note. I set the phone next to me on the comforter.

Now what? The moment had been amazing, but I didn't have any illusions it was meant to last beyond now. Did we say our goodbyes? Were we still playing the ARG as a team? Would we ignore each other once we left the room?

Evan traced the pads of my fingers with his thumb. "You've never done this before."

The kind tone, combined with the direct statement, sent pins prickling through me. Was he surprised? Disappointed? It didn't matter. I pushed out my casual bravado. "Of course I have. Haven't you?" I shouldn't have asked that. It bit into the pleasant fantasy and planted it in the middle of honest, blunt, non-playful reality.

Trevor's grip tightened on my thigh for the briefest of moments. "We, um..."

Evan paused in his attentions. "It's not like it's

something we make a habit of. The whole pictures thing? That was brand new and fucking hot. But, yeah, we've shared before."

Shared. The word rubbed me the wrong way, and I couldn't pinpoint why. Here I thought *never done this before* referred to a casual hook-up, not the fact we'd just made a Kathryn Sandwich. I didn't know what to do with the revelation.

Part of me had known the pickup was too smooth. Too easy, and it wasn't as if I thought I was either guy's first, but I couldn't ignore my disappointment that this hadn't been a completely unique, spontaneous moment. I drowned the sentiment. No reason to blow things out of proportion. Their past experience didn't change the fact this moment had been amazing, and I'd acted on the whim, not caring at the time about the details. As I repeated the reassurance, most of the gnawing in my stomach faded.

My phone chirped again, slicing through questions I didn't want to face. Another note from Jackson. *You sure?*

I studied the simple message with a frown. Jackson was as protective as any brother, but he'd never been a nag about it. Two words shouldn't concern me so much.

"Everything all right?" Evan righted himself and turned to face me.

God, he was gorgeous. And only for looking at, now on. I pulled my gaze from his defined chest before my eyes could drift lower, and directed it back at the device in my hand. "I think so." I replied to Jackson as well. *Unless you know something I don't, I'm fine.*

I didn't even have time to look up, before his response chimed through. *Then you're taking up modeling?* Huh? I stared at the cryptic words. What the hell? Seconds later I received a link, followed by, *Carter found these on some new stock photo site.*

A glance told me two pairs of eyes watched me with concern and curiosity. I gave a generic wave of my hand, not sure what it meant, and clicked Jackson's link. "What the…?" The faint words tumbled past my lips, and I trailed off. It was exactly what Jackson had said. The collage on the splash page had two pictures of me, taken that morning in the conference room downstairs. Several others on the site were from the convention too. I let myself linger on a touch of relief they were all from downstairs. Still…

I sent Jackson back an, *I don't know what this is. But it doesn't have my okay. Looking into it.*

Okay, his next message read. *Ping me if you need help.*

"Kitten?" The concern in Evan's voice dragged me back to the room.

Right. I wasn't alone. I wasn't sure what to say, so I handed him my phone. Trevor shifted his weight, to look over Evan's shoulder. "The fuck?" Evan said, as he handed the device back. "We just took those."

This wasn't good at all.

5

I wasn't going to panic over it. I knew the pictures taken downstairs would be made public—that was the entire point. However, I hadn't signed any sort of release with this site, or given them my permission in any way. In addition, those images were only posted an hour ago, and as part of some silly convention game. What kind of stock-photo site had to scan a ridiculous hashtag, to steal images for resale?

None of it made sense. I stood, lost in thought. All my concerns about whether or not the encounter with Trevor and Evan had been a bad idea tumbled to the back of my mind.

"Kathryn?" Trevor's voice cut through a mental speculation with no real direction. "Talk to us?

Correction—all my concerns about the shared moment between the three of us had vanished, except for one. "Those are your pictures." I found my top and bra draped over the back of a chair, and pulled both on. It wasn't an accusation, and I wasn't certain the images came from Trevor, but most of the other shots taken downstairs had someone posing next to me, or people in the background. Only Trevor and Evan's pics would be clean. Their pics from downstairs, anyway. My skin heated at the still-fresh images flooding my mind.

"They definitely look like mine." Trevor held up his phone and showed me a shot identical to the one on the newly-discovered site. Even though he'd made time to dig up a picture, both men still sat naked on the bed, watching me. I wasn't going to stare. More important things were going on than two naked human gods watching me have a meltdown. I fished my skirt from under the desk, but my panties were nowhere to be found. Fuck it. I was going to my room, anyway. I'd grab a new pair.

A new thought occurred to me, and as ridiculous as it was, I had to ask. If anyone got their hands of the pictures Trevor took up here… why didn't I think of that before he started snapping shots? "You weren't hacked, were you?" What if he'd pissed off a girlfriend they'd *shared,* and she had access to some account he synced his phone with, and oh God… I sank onto the edge of the bed. I'd been so stupid.

"I promise I wasn't." Trevor shifted until he sat next to me. "I don't sync the device, and not even Evan knows any of my login information. Your pictures are safe."

A paper-thin wisp of relief floated through me. "That's something." At least I had a valid reason to make a weak excuse and scoot my butt out of here. The thought of walking away for good echoed inside me, bouncing around and bruising my tentative grip on control. I had no idea why I was so reluctant to leave these two. I still knew nothing about them beyond that they were amazing in bed. Hardly the basis for a long term relationship of any kind.

Being spontaneous was one thing, but now I was irrational. Time to go. "Thank you for"—I waved my hand, not sure what to call it—"this. I need to go. Figure out how to contact whoever owns the site and get those pictures taken down."

"Kitten." Evan grabbed my wrist tightly enough to make me pause, but not so I couldn't break free if I wanted. "We're in this together."

His firm grip, the heat of his rough palm on my skin, re-summoned all my doubts and questions. Why? What did any of it have to do with them?

My question must have shown on my face. "They're my photos," Trevor said. "Also, as far as I can tell, there's no way to get a hold of anyone on this site. No form, no email, no phone. Not even a broken *Contact Us* link."

Wonderful. He had a point, about having a stake in this. He hadn't been violated the way I had, but it still wasn't right. "There are ways to look into domain ownership. Even locked and private information. My laptop is in my room. I can't do anything from here but stare at my phone."

"Then go grab your computer and meet us downstairs in half an hour." Evan let go of my hand. I tucked aside my sudden surge of longing. He stood, and it took the last of my willpower not to let my gaze drift over him and linger on his cock. I didn't quite succeed. I looked back up, to find a smile playing on his face. "We can all shower, get dressed—though don't feel obliged to change on our account"—he looked me over—"and find each other in the lobby."

He wasn't asking. I wanted to argue I could handle this alone and let them know what I found. The words struggled in the back of my mind, to force their way out. My mouth wasn't willing to surrender the chance to spend more time with them. "Half an hour. See you downstairs."

I had my hand on the door latch, when Trevor said, "Kathryn."

I whirled, to find him standing directly behind me. My breath caught at the close proximity. The sharp coolness of his body wash mingled with traces of sweat and sex, filling my head and making me wish this wasn't over. "What's up?" I was surprised I managed to keep my voice steady.

He planted a hand at the base of my neck and kissed me. I parted my lips, stunned by the abrupt gesture but enjoying every bit of it. Sinking into the hunger. His tongue accepted the opening and danced into my mouth. I pressed closer, into his bare form, wanting—needing—to feel his skin against mine. I dug my fingers into the sinewy strength of his arms. Clinging. Drowning. His rock hard cock dug into my hip. This wasn't fair. He shouldn't spark something so primitive and needy in me. Unlike with Evan and the control he exuded, this was a give and take. An equal struggle to dive into each other but still keep our distance.

Trevor broke the kiss but didn't let go. "I had to know what that felt like." He rested his forehead against mine, his voice low, meant only for me. He stepped back. "See you downstairs."

My head was a no-man's land of chaos, as I headed toward the elevator. With every step I took, the cool air brushed my bare mound, kissing the dampness and reminding me of what I'd done. The pleasant ache in my backside was a unique token of the morning as well. Years of instinct and indoctrination from the world around me insisted I should be ashamed. I didn't have any regrets, though. Well, maybe that it was only a one-time thing, but that was more of an unrealistic longing, to be stowed away under the amazing memories.

I barely registered the people around me, as I rode up to my floor and spilled into the hallway with a handful of other costumed folks. Several of them were bent over their phones, chattering. It was none of my business. My own life had gotten infinitely more interesting.

Back in my room, I stripped off my cosplay and

stepped into the shower. I kept things quick, to resist the temptation to dive into the memories one more time. To finish off what my body started when Trevor kissed me. I didn't need to rub myself raw.

I dried and dressed in cutoff shorts and a T-shirt. Suddenly the costumes I brought held too much meaning to be appealing. They carried both my desire to share them with the guys, and the irritation I felt at having my image stolen and posted online for the world to purchase.

I splashed cold water on my face, to force myself back to reality, shook away most traces of my euphoria from earlier, and headed back downstairs with my laptop bag slung over my shoulder. Now that I had dragged my head out of the clouds, I was more aware of the people around me. Several groups, most of them in costume, huddled around phones. I expected it to a point, but this felt wrong. Most I passed were grumbling and cursing, and some seemed on the edge of hysteria.

I planted myself in front of a group of three people. I only acknowledged in passing thought that I never would have been so bold this morning. "What's going on?" I asked.

One girl in black-and-white face makeup, and a red-and-black corset with more cleavage showing than I had boobs, looked up. "You were in the ARG room this morning. Right? We took your picture."

I nodded. "Are you looking at the photo site?"

"Check the hashtag." She showed me her phone.

"There's more than one. So far, people have found at least ten sites with their images on them."

The chaos in my skull merged with the bedlam and erupted into an anxiety that crawled through my nerves.

"Thanks." I was already walking toward the stairs, too impatient to wait for a car packed with people. One site was bad luck. More than ten, all in a few hours? The coincidence was beyond implausible. What the hell was going on? I wanted to get in front of my laptop and figure this out.

More whispers, grumbles, and very loud complaints reached me. Everyone involved was already doing everything I could do. Seeing who owned the domain, looking for contact information, finding Cease-and-Desist form letters online.

I paused midstride, as something occurred to me. Our pictures hadn't been stolen. This was the game. So what was the point? Chloe had mentioned software testing and security. Pieces clicked in my head. They wanted to see if people could find out who was behind this. I wasn't certain, but it seemed as good a lead as any.

I spun back to my room, to ditch my laptop. If everyone was busy online, I needed another approach. An angle nobody tried yet.

I kept half an eye on #RINARG, on my phone, and the rest of my attention on my surroundings as I wove through the lobby. The events online were the equivalent of a digital meltdown. People threatening to sue. Publicly crying about their families or coworkers seeing them in *that* costume. The most significant thing to me was the shared links about what had already been discovered. There was too much information to process while I walked. I paused and brushed my gaze over the faces around me. Evan and Trevor were nowhere to be found.

Something nudged my mind. A phrase just out of my grasp, but what was it? Words I'd heard earlier. *Twisting my head.* The thought fluttered on the edge of my consciousness.

"Hey, Kitten." Evan's breath caressed my cheek, and his arm settled against my back. "Miss us?"

Did I miss my random, impulsive fling? The

happy flutter beneath my ribs at their presence said *yes*.

Trevor stepped around us and headed toward a nearby sofa. He didn't meet my gaze until he took a seat. "Changed your mind on the computer?" His tone was cool, and his smile didn't quite reach his eyes.

Some of my giddiness faded. I needed to remember what happened upstairs was not the same as what we were doing now, and not interpret Evan's overt friendliness as anything more than that. "I don't think I'm going to need it."

Evan nudged me forward, dropped onto the far end of the same sofa Trevor occupied, and tugged my hand, prompting me to sit between them. I offered zero resistance. Cool reception or otherwise, my skin still hummed with the memories of being in the middle a short while ago.

"I looked for contact info while he showered." Evan leaned back and draped an arm on the couch behind me. "There's nothing out there. What made you back off?"

They didn't see it. I let a sliver of satisfaction slide in. "It doesn't matter. It's part of the game." I related everything I'd overheard and managed to glean in the halls. "My guess is, within the next half hour or so, someone will find whatever they're meant to, online, and Rinslet will own up to it being a clue."

Evan scowled. "So we sit back and let someone else get there first? Then what's the point?"

"Nope. We get our information another way." I pulled up a mobile version of the website for Rinslet's latest game. They had a massively multi-player online role-playing game in public beta testing. Based on the list of social features offered, I was almost certain the stock photo sites were an indirect way of testing their security. "One of you puts on your smoothest sweet talking voice, calls support, and coerces your way into finding out whatever it is we're supposed to know, to get the next clue."

"I like it." Evan pulled his phone from his pocket. "Tell me what I need to say."

Trevor shook his head. "Hang on. It won't be that simple. It's a good idea, but it's not going to work the way you think."

I frowned at being shot down so quickly, without a discussion, and defensiveness leaked into my voice. "Why not?"

He held up a hand. "It might. I'm not saying it's a bad idea. The thing is odds are pretty high we'll get a guy on the phone, if we call."

Being the only women on a team of twenty five at the call center I worked at, I knew he was right. Still, I wasn't sure why it mattered. "And?"

"And silver-tongued serpent or not, that seriously decreases the odds of Evan sweet talking his way into information."

"Oh." I sank back into the cushions with a sigh. "Never mind."

"It's still a good idea." Trevor shifted so he faced

me, and his knees brushed mine. "I'm thinking someone else needs to be the executioner."

Evan squeezed my shoulder. "You've got my vote. It's your idea, so you already know what to say. Right?"

My gut flopped in on itself. "I don't think I can."

"Why not?" Evan asked, no accusation in his voice. "You've got all the right skills."

I had a lot of bluffing and bullshit. But if I backed out now, they'd know I was faking this whole smooth-and-confident thing. I swallowed my nervousness. "All right. I'll call."

"You'll be brilliant," Evan whispered.

As I dialed the support number on the beta-testing website, I wished I had his confidence. Each ring in my ear was like another chime on my death march. The idea sounded so much more brilliant when someone else had to pull it off.

"Thank you for calling Rinslet Beta Support. My name is Grant. How can I help you?" The voice on the other end of the line spoke so quickly, words all running together, it took me a second to process what he'd said.

I shook off the confusion, dragged up self-assured me, and prayed whatever came out of my mouth wouldn't be stupid. "Hey, Grant." Wow, did I really sound this breathy on the phone? I needed to roll with it, not overthink it. "I'm hoping you can help me. I'm one of the testers for the new game, and"—I gave a tiny sigh—"it's giving me some trouble."

A long pause grew between us, and for a moment I was worried he'd hung up. "Sure." His reply came sharply and abruptly, startling me. "I just need some basic information. What's your character name?"

"I… What?" I knew exactly what he was asking, but I figured pretending I thought I was in the right place would help my cause. "I don't think we're talking about the same game. This is Rinslet Testing Support, right?"

Evan snickered, and I glared at him, willing him to be silent.

"Of course," Grant said. "But the only game we have in testing right now is *The Hoarde Online*."

"Oh, my God." It turned out, if I let the words roll, they came pretty easily. "I love *The Hoarde*. I mean…" I trailed off. I realized I was twirling a strand of hair around my finger, even though he couldn't see me. Trevor closed his hand over mine and shook his head with a smile. I rolled my eyes and turned my attention to the phone call. "Don't think I'm pervy or anything, but Darla, in number three… that part of the game where she's proving to her boyfriend she can keep up?"

"Yeah?" Grant said.

"So hot. I mean, she's gorgeous. Is it okay if I say that?"

Yes, Evan mouthed at me, looking like it was taking all his restraint not to laugh.

"Best. Scene. Ever." Grant's enthusiasm was almost tangible.

"Right?" I was really getting into this. It was kind of fun, to be honest. "Chloe Nielson is here. She was the head writer on that, wasn't she? Total girl-crush on her."

"Uh…" Grant trailed off. "Here, where?"

"She runs the game I'm helping test. They told you about that, right? I mean, do I need to talk to someone else? I like talking to you, Grant. I'm really hoping you can help me."

"No, of course I can. Whatever you need. What's going on?"

"It's just…" I chewed on my bottom lip. Trevor ran a finger along the flesh and pulled it away from my teeth, his brows raised. I stuck my tongue out at him. "I had this email address—to get a hold of her, you know? And I swore I put it in my phone, and now I can't find it anywhere. Can you give it to me?"

"Of course." Grant rattled off Chloe's contact information.

I traded a few more quips with him about *The Hoarde,* and gave him a friendly *thank you* before hanging up.

"God, you are fantastic, Kitten." Evan threw his head back with a barking laugh. "Absolutely brilliant."

"I second that," Trevor said.

I was already typing an email out to Chloe, including the guys' user names in the message and letting her know we could issue a formal Cease-and-Desist to Rinslet to take the photo sites down, but we were hoping it wasn't necessary. As an afterthought, I added *PS— Grant says hi.*

Within moments, I had a reply, congratulating us on being the first to crack the clues, telling me the sites would all be gone within minutes, and implying they hadn't even thought to check security on the Tech Support side of things. She wrapped it up by letting me know they were giving everyone else new clues, and the next phase of the game would start in the morning.

"Well?" Two pairs of eyes watched, expectantly.

I read Chloe's email out loud. "As of now, we're in the lead."

"Fuck, yeah!"

I was surrounded by cheers, high fives and hugs. I sank into it all, lingering on the happiness. This was so much fun. It was a shame it wouldn't last once the con was over. There was no way I could keep this up twenty-four-seven. I might as well enjoy it now.

Evan and Trevor didn't seem to be in a hurry to get anywhere else. The three of us hung out, hit up various panels, and wandered through the Dealers' Room more times than I could count. I'd never had so much fun doing random things. Innuendo and jokes flowed between us. It seemed like no topic was off limits, and that included quantum theory and whether or not Hentai—animated Japanese porn—was a legitimate art form.

The clock crept toward five, and then the afternoon blasted into evening. None of us mentioned going our separate ways, and with no real lags in conversation, I wasn't going to be the one to cut things short. We took a break from the crowds, to stroll a few blocks and grab dinner at a tiny place Trevor swore had the best Tiramisu in existence. I had to agree, and it wasn't only because it was too fun taking turns feeding each other. I tried to ignore the fading light outside, and that it meant this day would end sooner rather than later.

My phone buzzed with a text from Jackson. *Never heard back. You're good?*

I frowned at the message, guilt marring my good mood. *I'm sorry. I should have let you know. It was just a game, apparently. Explain more when you get here.*

His reply came through a moment later. *About that… Zoe's working late. We don't want to go without her. See you there tomorrow?*

Totally. I couldn't ignore my ambivalence. On the one hand, I'd been looking forward to hanging out with Jackson, his boyfriend Carter, and their girlfriend Zoe. On the other, if they weren't here, I didn't have to choose who to spend time with.

Evan covered my hand with his. That seemed to be his default—a hint of contact here, a light touch there. I didn't mind. "Everything okay?" he asked.

"It's all good." I grabbed my smile. Might as well focus on the positive. "My friends can't make it until tomorrow."

"So no one's going to notice if we kidnap you?" he asked with a teasing grin.

I painted on a wide-eyed look of shock. "Oh no, mister. Are you going to steal me away and tie me up and do naughty things to me?" Actually, I liked the sound of that.

He ducked in and brushed my earlobe with his lips. "Only if you beg." His voice was low and husky.

My laughter died in my throat when I met

Trevor's narrow-eyed gaze. His scowl vanished in an instant, expression going blank. Had I done something wrong? I was taking things too far, and he was tired of me. Nothing else made sense. Not anything else I was willing to believe. It definitely wasn't jealousy. Evan was friendly, but I had no illusions this meant more to either of them than a bit of fun and distraction.

Evan sank back into his seat, breaking all contact with me. "The truth this time. This is a first for you."

At least now I understood what he was talking about. I could deny it again, but they already suspected otherwise. That, and temporary relationship or not, I didn't want to keep building secrets on lies. "Being picked up by two gorgeous guys? Taken back to their room. Ravaged? This is a first."

"You don't seem to have a problem with it," Trevor said.

"Should I?" Besides the complete unlikeliness of it happening, the entire thing had been amazing. It still was.

Evan studied me. "Some people do."

"Not the people who say yes, I hope." I winced as the words slipped out. I didn't want the reminder this wasn't special.

Trevor drummed his fingers on the table. "Actually… Those people. Yes. I mean, it's all consensual and they enjoy it as far as I can tell, until it comes time to admit to anyone else what they've done."

"That sucks." I couldn't think of a better way to

phrase it. "Why go participate if you're not cool with it?"

Trevor turned away, fiddling with his straw.

Evan clenched his jaw and paused for a moment before responding. "Fantasy fulfillment. Right? No one actually has three person relationships."

"Sure they do."

Two heads snapped in my direction, eyes wide. "Not in real life," Trevor said.

"Yes, in real life." For a couple of guys who shared women for fun, they were a little closed-minded. "My brother has a boyfriend and a girlfriend."

Trevor shook his head and gave a snort. "And they know about each other?"

"They all live together. Happily." Jackson didn't mind discussing his relationship, but I didn't like the questions with underlying hints of judgement. Especially given how Evan and Trevor spent their morning. As in, fucking me.

"Really?" Evan's tone held no disbelief. His expression was open, and his tone curious.

Trevor frowned. "That's three people out of millions. I'm not saying I have a problem with it, but their experience doesn't make it status quo, or even likely anywhere else."

"Anyway." Evan's voice was clipped—a sharp contrast to seconds ago. "What's next?"

Trevor shrugged. "Whatever."

A chill from the air conditioner sped down my spine. Or I was pretty sure that's what caused me to shiver. "Viewing room?" I tried to keep my tone light, wanting to go back to the fun we'd been having before the conversation turned serious.

They exchanged a look I couldn't interpret, with Trevor's lips drawn into a thin line, and creases marring Evan's forehead.

A buzz broke the bizarre staring match, and Trevor grabbed his phone from his pocket. "Fuck." He scowled at the device.

"Work?" Evan asked.

And like that, the tension vanished. Or maybe it had never been there, and I was paranoid.

Trevor nodded, scrolling through something on screen. "Servers crashed. Night guy can't get them back online. May have to drive to the data center."

The words had meaning to me, but only barely. Their biggest significance was the reminder we all had lives outside this pocket of reality we'd built around ourselves.

He pushed away from the table and stood, scowl stamped on his face. "This might take a while. I'm sorry."

"Hey." Evan nodded at something behind Trevor.

"Sure." Trevor pressed his phone to his ear, and seconds later, stepped outside.

I felt like I missed something significant. "What was that about?"

"If he has to drive out to where the machines are, he'll be a couple of hours. He'll meet us when he's done." Evan offered me his hand. "That is, unless you want to call it a night."

"Not without you." The words were bolder than I expected from myself, but they tasted right. I placed my palm in his and stood. What would it be like to have the kind of connection with someone, that an entire conversation could be conveyed in a couple of words and a tilt of the head? Evan didn't let go of my hand right away, but when we stepped outside, his fingers drifted from mine. We meandered down the streets.

"Where are you from?" he asked. "What lucky city claims you, when the weekend is over?"

The way he phased the question filled me with a pleasant glow. Then again, most of what Evan said to me sounded both flattering and sincere. "I'll be heading back to a town a whole ten or fifteen minutes away. I'm local."

"Really?" If it was possible for a single word to embody the term *pleasantly surprised,* he'd pulled it off perfectly. "Us too."

My pulse leaped in my veins. That meant seeing them after the weekend was a possibility. I shelved the thought quickly, but not before disappointment set in with the reminder this wasn't what we had. "So getting a room makes it easier to pick up…" My question died in my throat. I didn't want to hear his answer. Well, the morbid part of me did, but the rest of me already knew I was just a random girl in the right place.

Evan glanced at me, expression unreadable. "No." His refusal sounded as sincere as everything else he'd said. "It was so… uh…" He looked away. "Because it's more convenient than heading home at night. You know?"

"I do know. Me too." So why did it feel like the one thing he'd said today that wasn't one-hundred-percent honest?

Silence descended over us. I turned my attention to my feet. Small talk had never been my forte.

"Is Trevor in IT?" I blurted out the first question that popped into my mind. When I didn't get a response, I glanced sideways, to see Evan studying me.

He smiled and looked away, shoving his hands in his pockets. "He is. Director for a little start-up that makes web applications."

"That's cool." Way to be witty, me. This hadn't exactly opened the floodgate of conversation I hoped for. Except, now that I'd broached the subject, I wanted to know more about both these men whose lives I'd dropped into for a day. "What do you do?"

He relaxed his shoulders and seemed to walk straighter. "I'm a Materials' Process and Physics Technical Analyst, at Boeing."

My mind ground to a stop, stuttering on the words. I got the basics of what Trevor did—I was telephone support for networking hardware. Whatever Evan just said had no bearing in my world. I'd expected him to say Sales, or something along those lines. That was what I got for making assumptions. "I… What?"

His chuckle had the same lighthearted feeling as earlier. At least he was over the weird tension. "I'm a chemical engineer, and I work with the compounds they use for planes."

Oh. "That sounds infinitely more genius-level than… Well, anything, really."

"It's not." He settled a hand at the small of my back, to point me toward the intersection. His touch lingered, and warmth from his palm spread over my skin. "It's just a different way of looking at the world."

"Standing on my head is a different way of looking at the world." I realized he'd been the one leading the conversation about quantum physics, earlier. Something told me he was a lot smarter than he let on. It wasn't that he acted stupid; it was that never once during the entire day had he talked down to anyone.

"It's true. It is." He glided his hand along my back and hooked it on my hip, pulling me closer. The gesture felt natural, and I leaned into him. We slowed our pace to make it easier to walk that way. "But the job is what I have a knack for. It's cool, but it doesn't make me special. What do you do?"

Things way too boring and trite, compared to a guy who designed stuff for planes. "Tech support." My answer came out flat.

"You don't like it?"

"It's not bad."

"But it's not great. What would you rather be doing?"

My instinct was to keep my answers short. To redirect the conversation back to him. Except he sounded genuinely interested. "Teaching."

"As in, school? High-school kids or something?"

Embarrassment flooded me. "Aikido."

"Really?" The single word exuded curiosity. "That's really cool. You must be amazing, to be able to teach."

"I'm a black-belt. I think I'm pretty good." My sensei said I had a natural talent for it, but saying so felt like bragging.

We reached the hotel, stepped out of the flow of traffic, and paused in the lobby. I wasn't ready for this night to end. Evan faced me but never broke contact. Admiration shone on his face. "That's wicked. I bet you're better than you let on. Why don't you do that, then? Are the jobs hard to get?"

I didn't do *that,* because I was too shy to stand in front of a class and teach. I'd thought I could do it, but I flopped fantastically during my interview audition. Completely froze, in front of a group of new students. I couldn't admit that to Evan, though. "I'm not good enough to ne an instructor."

He traced his fingers lightly down my arm. "You're being modest."

"There's no way you can know that." I desperately wanted the conversation to focus on anything but me.

I didn't mind the attention—I couldn't think of the last time anyone was so interested in hearing about my life, and it made me feel wonderfully gooey inside. But if we talked about it much longer, I had a feeling I'd have to keep making things up, to hold his interest, and temporary relationship or not, I didn't like the idea of deceiving him. "Did you have to go to school for your job? I mean, of course you did."

"Yup." His mouth twisted, and he studied me. "Five years, Master's of Science. I did a little sparring in Basic, but nothing as intensive as aikido."

And now we were back on me. "Basic. As in… You were in the army."

"Four years. It's how I paid for college. And learned to work on and fly helicopters. Would you show me some of what you know?"

The request knocked me off guard. "What? Like, now?"

"Sure." He tugged my fingers. "Hotel's got a workout room with yoga mats. Show me a couple of throws or tumbles?"

He was a foot taller than me and had to be at least fifty pounds heavier, and he wanted me to show him some throws? "I'm not really dressed for it."

"Nothing intensive." He pulled me toward the exercise room. "Unless you really don't want to."

Did I? The answer rushed to me more quickly than I expected, almost bowling over my thoughts. "I'd definitely like to."

The room was empty. At least that was something.

I set my shoes by the edge of the pads, and he mimicked my actions. My heart hammered in my chest with both fear and excitement. I wanted to impress him, but I also didn't want anyone to get hurt.

I moved to the center of one of the workout spot, and he hovered at the edge, watching. I grabbed his hand and pulled him closer, then spun so he was behind me. He wrapped his arm around my neck and pressed into my back, and a shock of familiarity raced through me. "I like this kind of demonstration," he purred, lips touching the back of my neck.

It would be easy to say *forget it*. Sink into his touch. The temptation surged inside, and I pushed it back. Easy, but somehow also not right, with only the two of us here. "Relax your posture," I said.

"Yes, Sensei." His tone shifted to business in an instant.

I situated my hands on his arms. "This is a little more advanced than what we teach beginners, but you said you've done some sparring. Do you know how to roll?"

"As in, tuck myself into a ball and tumble, so I don't get hurt? I've got some idea."

"Good." I resisted the urge to press back into him and drown in his touch. "I'm going to go slowly. When I toss you forward, fall into the momentum."

"You're going to toss me?" Disbelief crept into his question.

"Yup." Without warning, I shifted my weight,

planted my feet, and altered my stance to turn my own body into a fulcrum. I felt him falter behind me, and I used his weight and uncertainty to bring him over my shoulder.

He hit the mat with an *oof* but rolled into the gesture.

I rested my toes on his chest. "Point for me."

He brushed my leg aside and climbed to his feet. "That was fantastic. Never saw it coming. I have to know how you did it. I mean, I get the physics, but show me again."

We spent the next half hour repeating the move, with him trying it several times until he was happy. And then I sped it up to full pace. I had him rush me from behind, and planted him on the floor. I straddled him, hands on his wrists, to hold them above his head, both of us laughing.

"You were wrong, you know." His voice dropped an octave, brown eyes searching my face. "You're a fantastic instructor. If someone told you otherwise, you need to find a new dojo."

"Thanks." I flushed at the compliment and the closeness of his body. It would be so easy to lean in and steal a kiss. So tempting… I crammed the thought aside, stood, and offered him a hand up.

He didn't let go of my hand when he was on his feet. "Do you have anywhere to be?" he asked.

"Not really. They're running a Kurosawa marathon all night on the hotel convention channel. That was my only plan."

"So come watch in our room." He squeezed my hand.

As we made our way upstairs, I wondered what the rules were about staying friends with a fling after it was over. That was probably a stupid idea, but as I glanced at Evan, I couldn't help entertaining the thought.

8

The door creaked open, and Trevor stepped into the room. When his gaze landed on us —me half-sitting, half-lying on Evan, both of us propped up against the headboard—a shadow passed over his face. He shook his head, dropped his phone on the nightstand, and sank onto the edge of the bed. His attention stayed on the TV when he asked, "Did I miss the fun?" It sounded as if he was trying to be upbeat, but his words fell flat.

I'd enjoyed my time with Evan, but Trevor wasn't talking about that. Honestly, while getting physical had been a background thought, it never became more during the evening. I'd been focused on other things.

"We wouldn't start anything without you," Evan sat, disentangling himself from me in the process.

I scooted a little further away, an uneasy pit

forming in my gut. I almost felt guilty, as if I'd been caught doing something I shouldn't. The thought didn't make any sense, and I dismissed it. "Is everything better at work?"

"For now." Trevor finally looked at us again.

"You fixed it with your massive, impressive brain?" I drawled out each word with teasing innuendo.

The shadows melted from his expression and were replaced with hesitant amusement. "I don't know if I'd call it impressive."

"You're being modest." I winked.

"The woman's got good taste in"—Evan cleared his throat—"brains."

"She's not a zombie." Trevor's shoulders relaxed.

"I might be. Or maybe I just have a solid appreciation for a nice organ."

Trevor leaned back and planted his palms on the mattress behind him. "I'm more than a sexy brain."

Evan scooted closer to me. "At the risk of shattering all this innuendo, *God,* I'd love to watch you suck his cock, Kitten."

Arousal rushed through me at the direct request, flooding my skin and drawing my nipples to hard nubs. That escalated quickly. Then again, I didn't have any illusions about why I was in their room. I looked at Trevor and licked my bottom lip.

He shifted his hips. "You won't get an argument from me."

Gaze never leaving Trevor's, I slid from the bed and crawled the short distance to where he sat. Still on my knees, I glided my hand up the inside of his thigh. Desire unfurled in my belly, and Trevor groaned when I caressed his bulge. I stroked him through his jeans. His lips parted, and he closed his eyes. With each new touch, I was intensely aware we weren't alone. Evan's breathing grew heavy behind me, making the dampness between my legs spread. I moved higher and undid Trevor's jeans.

I freed his cock, and it jerked against my hand when I wrapped my fingers around the smooth skin. The air around me hummed with anticipation. Every time I shifted my weight, the seam of my shorts rubbed against my swollen clit. I flicked my tongue over the bulbous head. Trevor sucked in a sharp breath through his teeth. I pumped while I licked tight circles along his shaft. When I took him in my mouth, I swore my whimper matched his gasp. I had to keep my hand in place, to prevent him from thrusting down my throat.

He thrust his hips toward my face. I squeezed my legs together, as the throbbing between my thighs intensified. The little movements were enough to tease me, sending satin over my nipples and denim pressing into my sex, but I wanted relief for the intense sensations.

Trevor tangled his fingers in my hair, holding my head in place. I looked up again, to find him watching me, pale eyes wide. His breath came in jagged pants, chest heaving each time I slid my lips along his cock.

A hand—Evan's; that would make sense—palmed my ass, then pushed between my legs. He pressed my clothing into my slit. Massaging my ache. I groaned against Trevor, the vibrations running into my touch. Trevor jerked against me, breathing growing shallow. Evan massaged harder, stroking me and drawing out my pleasure. Every gasp, grunt, and sigh bounced in my mind, blurring my thoughts.

"I want to watch him come in your mouth," Evan said.

"No. Not like this." Trevor spoke as if forcing the words through gravel. He jerked from my grasp and yanked me to my feet. Before I could push out a question, or even figure out what I should say, he crushed his mouth to mine, desperate and hungry. He only broke away long enough to tear my shirt over my head and fling it aside. Desperation welled inside, consuming me. I couldn't get close enough. I sought purchase, digging my fingers into his solid arms.

Evan grabbed my hips, and then scraped his fingers forward to pop the button on my cutoffs, and drag down my zipper. Trevor deepened the kiss. He massaged my breast through my bra, pinching and kneading. Pulling groans from me. Too many sensations demanded my focus, and I wanted to absorb every one. I wrapped my fingers around Trevor's cock again, stroking in time to the bump and grind between the three of us.

The sharp scent of fresh soap mingled with the musk of cologne and sex. Trevor kissed down my neck, sucking the skin, nipping with his teeth, drawing the sting of pleasure to the surface. Evan dipped under my panties and dove for my folds. I mewled when he found my clit, struggling to find my breath as he circled the swollen nub.

My legs wobbled, but two sturdy bodies kept me upright. Trevor increased the attention to my nipples, thrusting his hips in time with my hand. Evan's dick pressed into my ass, insistent even through our clothes. I ground against his fingers. Waves rolled through me, building and battling for release. Orgasm crashed over me, and I cried out, riding every feeling.

Before my climax could ebb, Evan yanked my shorts to the ground.

"I need to fuck you." Trevor's voice was strained, and his eyes were wide, making him look as unwoven as I felt. He jerked his shirt over his head, then shed his jeans and kicked them aside.

"God, yes. Please." I wasn't in the mood for that kind of drawn-out teasing. His bare skin against mine was heat and ice, soothing my desire and stoking the flames.

He grasped my hips, spun us both, and nudged me onto the bed. He fell on top of me, hands on either side of my head.

"Condom," I managed, hating the necessity.

Trevor gave a shaky laugh. "You're going to kill me."

Evan handed him a foil package.

Trevor fumbled, before extracting the rubber and rolling it on. He searched my face one last time, and then thrust inside me. I arched my back at the harsh penetration, almost coming again when he plunged deep.

Evan stood next to the bed, dick in his hand, stroking fast. I tilted my head to the side and licked the head. Trevor pushed my knees forward, slamming against my G-spot. I gripped the sheets in my fists, needing something to grab, to keep from drowning in the moment.

"Oh, God." Evan increased his pace, and a stream of white—warm and sticky—spurted across my chest and face.

Trevor's grunts became more punctuated. Staccato bursts of enjoyment. He dropped one of my legs and pressed his thumb to my clit. With him fingering me, I came again, grinding against his pelvis, riding out the torrent flooding me. My pussy spasmed and clenched around his cock.

He gasped and shuddered. I knew it was impossible even if he weren't wearing a condom, but I swore I felt him spill inside me. He slowed, and then stopped.

Silence blanketed the room but didn't mute the energy still buzzing in the air. Adrenaline still rushed through me, but my waning pleasure kissed away some of the excess. I wasn't sure how we'd gone so quickly from playful teasing to frantic fucking. My mind wasn't in the right place to puzzle it out, too happy to drift along on euphoric clouds.

No way would any con experience ever top this one. It didn't matter what happened after tonight. I needed to believe that.

9

A barely-there noise scraped into my drifting consciousness and dragged me awake. Where was I? Something weighed on my hip. Evan's arm. Right. I'd fallen asleep in their room. My gaze fell on the other bed. Blankets tossed aside. Sheets twisted. Pillows in disarray. Trevor hadn't slept next to us. I don't know if that made me sadder, or if it was the fact he wasn't there now.

It was true I'd known them for less than a day, but Evan seemed to wear most of his feelings near the surface. Trevor was harder for me to read, though. I wasn't sure why that gnawed at me. Why it mattered at all. Once the con was over, we'd all go back to real life, most likely never to stumble on each other again in this city packed full of people.

Knowing that didn't silence my nagging curiosity. I disentangled myself from Evan, careful not to wake him, and swung my legs over the edge of the bed. It wasn't hard to figure out where Trevor was. The only sources of light in the room came from under the door to the hallway and from the curtain leading out the balcony. Trevor stood outside, attention directed at the city, jeans hanging low on his hips and nothing covering his torso.

I scanned the room for my discarded clothing, and finally glimpsed a T-shirt the same color as mine. It draped halfway down my thighs when I pulled it on, and I looked down. Apparently, this was Trevor's. Would he mind? Again, it was so difficult to tell with him. There were moments when we clicked and everything we did felt intimate—even swapping random movie quotes. Other times I swore he built a wall of ice between us. I didn't want to take the shirt off. It was selfish, but being wrapped in something smelling so distinctly of him settled my rambling thoughts.

I stepped outside and closed the door behind me. He didn't look back at the soft swish of glass sliding in its frame. His knuckles paled as he gripped the safety rail in front of him, but he didn't speak.

Maybe I shouldn't be out here. I didn't know what to say. Breaking the stillness felt like a violation.

"Have you ever been to L.A.?" His low voice merged with the calm instead of shattering it.

"Once." I stepped next to him, both to see what he was looking at and to hear him better. "Anime Expo, a few years ago."

He gave a short laugh. "Us too. First time we did

this. She didn't stick around after. None of us were interested."

A raw ache grew in my throat. Was that a hint? Snippets of the day raced through my mind, from their insistence we still meet up to talk about what turned out to be the ARG, to dinner, to the second invitation back to their room. I might not be the boldest person, but I wasn't completely oblivious about the world around me. Despite Trevor's flashes of hot and cold, I didn't think this was his way of telling me to leave. I wasn't sure how to respond.

"It was his idea." Trevor raked his fingers through his hair. "Not that I took much convincing. I'm a guy. I don't mind kink, I love sex, and the environment was right. People live different lives at cons. Step outside their shells. Let their guard down."

I knew this all too well.

Trevor turned to face me, and a smile cracked his somber expression. His gaze traveled over me. "Nice shirt." An edge lined his voice.

"It was dark. It's what I grabbed. I hope that's okay."

"It's fine. Better than fine. You look incredible."

Heat flooded my skin. "Thanks."

He stepped behind me, fixed his hands on my hips, and pointed me toward the city. "Do you see that?"

I looked out over the view. A million tiny lights, like stars on the ground, twinkling until they reached the mountains and faded into blackness. Something told me he was looking for a more specific answer than that. "See what?" I asked.

"In L.A. it didn't matter if it was two in the morning. There was always traffic. The roads were never empty. We're smack dab in the middle of downtown Salt Lake City, and you can only see maybe ten cars from here. It's quiet, it's unassuming, and it's calm. But people don't want to live here. They want to live in Hollywood. Places like this are boring."

"I think it's pretty. I love the way the valley looks at night."

He slid his palms forward, until his fingers interlocked and rested on my stomach. I leaned back into him, and he set his chin on the top of my head. A tiny voice told me this was too intimate for the relationship we had. I ignored it. Everything about this moment was right for now.

"Me too." His chest rose and fell against my spine when he sighed. "I always thought it looked like the sky, but upside down."

I sank further into his embrace, a new kind of warmth filling me when his words synced up so well with my thoughts. "When I was little, one Fourth of July we drove up to the very top streets in The Aves, to watch the fireworks." The moment from my past sparked in my mind, happy and bright, tinged with a sprinkle of bittersweet because it was one of the few holidays Dad was able to take off and spend with us. "When it was all over, we stayed up there for a while. My dad didn't want to deal with traffic." I had no idea why I was sharing the memory. It was something I never talked about, even with Jackson. An idea I'd tucked away long ago. Telling Trevor felt right. The relaxed arms holding me, the way his breathing matched mine, and the stillness of the night drew the words out. "I remember looking out over it all and wondering, if I grew up to be an astronaut, would the sky look like that when I was actually a part of it?"

"I did something similar when I was little"—his lips moved against my hair, his voice low and soothing—"except I was going to be an X-Wing pilot."

A tiny laughed slipped past my lips. "I'm being serious."

"So am I." His chuckle destroyed any attempt at indignation. "There was no way Luke Skywalker was a better Jedi than me."

I rested my hands on his. "I wouldn't fly an X-Wing. I'd want a Bebop."

"I think that's the ship's name. Not what kind it is. But I won't argue the technicalities of a cartoon. You'd be a space cowboy, huh? Fae?"

I didn't want to be the sexy hustler in the skimpy yellow leather from *Cowboy Bebop*. I wanted to be the smart hacker girl everyone underestimated. "Ed." I adored that he knew what I was talking about without explanation and at the same time hadn't gone hardcore fanboy about my possible misrepresentation of the show. In fact, nothing about the moment left me wanting.

"Brilliant, lost, independent hacker girl, who

doesn't care what anyone thinks of her. I can see that. Does that mean you need to be found?"

"Depends on who's looking for me."

The conversation slipped from one topic to the next. A shared stream of consciousness with seemingly no end in sight. I didn't know how many hours passed, but light was pushing the dark from the sky when I yawned for the third time in as many minutes.

"We should sleep." He sounded disappointed.

Or I was projecting. Both, probably. "I suppose."

He let go of me enough to lead us inside. He studied me again, brows pinched and an unreadable emotion darkening his eyes. With a shake of his head, he dropped my hand. The loss of contact was an icy shock to my system. I tangled my fingers in his before he could fall into his bed. "Don't," I whispered, not wanting to wake up Evan.

Trevor raised his brows, and a sad smile flashed over his face before vanishing. "Why not?" His question barely reached me.

I pressed closer. "Because then I have to choose." The quiet words echoed in my head as loudly as a scream, carrying more meaning than I intended. Far more significance than I wanted them to.

He planted his hands at the small of my back, dipped his head, and brushed his lips over my cheek. "Then choose me."

Three simple words. We were only talking about where to sleep for a single night. I looked up at him.

"Please?" I wasn't even sure what I was asking, but this didn't make it any less important he understand.

"Only for you." Using his entire frame, he pushed me back a step, toward Evan's bed. I couldn't help my smile as I slid between the sheets, next to a sleeping Evan. Trevor joined me and drew me close, my back to his chest and his head resting against mine.

A flood of warmth and acceptance blanketed me, singing in my joints and dancing under my skin. I'd never connected with anyone the way I did with Trevor. And while it was completely different with Evan, the bond with him felt just as strong. I was being sucked in by best friends, who were only looking for a random hookup at a convention. Who, as time wore on, made it very clear this was the only time they shared. I needed to lock away my reactions soon, or at the end of the weekend I would be moping over something I had no right to miss.

Evan stirred but didn't open his eyes. He reached out and covered my hand with his.

Trevor slid his palm under my shirt and settled it on my bare hip. "Goodnight, my amazing Kathryn." His whispered words sank into my thoughts.

If I didn't get a handle on this now, my psyche was going to be fucked. I refused to give credence to the ache in my chest, the dull throb telling me my heart wouldn't fare so well either.

"That's not what I'm saying." The muffled shout jarred me awake.

I jolted upright, as my surroundings slammed into focus. I sat in an empty bed, and Evan and Trevor stood on the balcony. My fuzzy thoughts told me that was probably Evan yelling.

"It sounds like it to me." Trevor's voice was just as loud.

I blinked bleary-eyed at the digital clock next to me. Seven in the morning. On a Saturday. The hotel guests had to be loving this. An invisible fist squeezed my chest, as I studied their faces through the glass, both twisted with fury.

Evan clenched his fists. "Because you're not fucking listening."

"Or you're talking over my head."

"I'm done here, until you pull your head out of your ass." Evan spun away and flung the door open.

He paused, one foot in the room, when he saw me. He clenched his jaw, then shook his head and strode past, floor shaking with each step. Seconds later, the door slammed shut behind him.

Concern flooded me. I was on my feet in an instant, not caring I still only wore a shirt. I blocked Trevor's path when he came back inside. "What's going on?"

Trevor stepped around me and grabbed a new T-shirt from a duffel bag on the floor, never looking directly at me. "Don't worry about it."

The casual brush-off stung. "Don't do that. I obviously am worried about it." It was easier than admitting the shrug-off left an empty pit inside me.

He met my gaze. "I have to leave the con early. Whatever happened last night at work isn't fixed after all." His jaw was clenched, and he wouldn't make eye contact.

"So that makes the two of you shout at the top of your lungs, first thing in the morning?"

Trevor's nostrils flared, and the corners of his eyes tugged down. "Don't push this, Kathryn. It is what it is, and having a long, drawn-out discussion isn't going to change that."

Whatever happened between us last night, the shared moments on the balcony seemed to be nonexistent now. The realization added a new sting to his dismissal, but I couldn't help bargaining anyway. Even though I knew his going back to work wasn't at the root of what had happened, it was all I had. "Can you fix it and come back? Get someone else to work on it remotely?"

God, I was pathetic. He already told me to let it go, and it wasn't as though any relationship with either of them was going to last past this weekend. Why did I push so hard?

"No. That won't fix anything." He tossed his clothes in his bag. "Keep the shirt. You wear it better than I do. I'm sorry I can't help you finish the game."

"I don't care about the fucking game!" My retort burst out louder than I expected, and I bit the inside of my cheek. "I care about…" I couldn't force the word out, even though it was right on the tip of my tongue. All I had to say was *you.* Except something told me it wouldn't make this better.

"Yeah. Me too. That's the problem."

My heart felt like it might crumple in on itself, and I couldn't find a response.

He shook his head and hooked his bag over his shoulder. "We all knew what this was." The fight was gone from his voice, as was all emotion. "I enjoyed every minute of it, but the weekend is over for me. If you run into Evan, whatever you say to him is between the two of you."

He felt the same way I did. Defiance burst forward. I couldn't let him leave like this. I wished Evan were here too, but I had to start somewhere. "Trevor, I don't want—"

"Stop." He spoke through gritted teeth. "Whatever you're going to say, don't. It's been twenty-four hours. We don't know each other, and in a few days, you'll be glad you kept this to yourself."

He was wrong. Keeping my mouth shut wasn't the answer. Except, his certainty knocked mine off-kilter. They didn't know me. I wasn't some bold, outgoing, fun person. I wore a mask, to make the day more enjoyable. What if they did the same—either or both of them? Even if they didn't, and if did actually had any fraction of the same feelings I did, it wasn't for the real me. My protests died, choked off in my tight throat.

He turned away. "I have to go."

CHLOE EMAILED ME WITH THE NEXT CLUE WHILE I WAS showering, and I tried to ignore the unreasonable ache inside when I sent her a quick note saying, *Sorry, have to bow out.* Trevor's shirt taunted me from the bathroom counter, where I'd tossed it. I hovered my fingers over it, tempted to put it back on, but I'd managed to mostly replace the scent of his cologne with body wash. I couldn't dive back into that unrealistic memory. That didn't stop me from tucking the shirt into my luggage.

I wandered the convention, unsure where I was going or what I wanted to do. As the top of each hour rolled around, I hovered near a panel, sometimes drifting into the room and then deciding I wasn't in the mood after all. Logic and reason sided with Trevor's words, asking why I let this get to me.

"Hey, Sis." Jackson startled me, as he fell into step beside me and draped an arm over my shoulders. "Did we miss anything interesting?"

Yup. Me being impulsive and doing things I knew better than to do. It wasn't that I regretted the time spent with Evan and Trevor, just that I'd started to believe it meant more than it did. "Not really," I said.

Carter held up a bag. "We brought lunch."

The smell of Chinese food wafted toward me, and my stomach growled in response, reminding me I'd skipped breakfast and it was almost two.

"Sorry we took so long." Zoe stood on my other side. Being surrounded by friends helped push my wallowing to the back of my mind, and dragged me to the surface. "Traffic, errands… Blah, blah, blah."

"You're not answering your phone." Concern leaked into Jackson's voice. "We almost ate without you." He spun me to face him, his brow furrowed. "Are you sure you're okay?"

I forced a smile onto my face and nodded toward the elevators. "Fine. Why do you keep asking me that?" I knew my laugh sounded forced. Jackson would see right through it. With any luck, he'd let it slide, though. What I needed right now was to pretend to be happy, to get over the fact I was no longer pretending to be fun. "Come up to my room. I'm starved."

Jackson studied me. "You've been so engrossed in

this thing"—he nodded at our surroundings—"you forgot to eat *and* ignored your phone? Guess you are fine."

"See?" I half dragged him toward the elevators, and his partners followed. They kept up a steady stream of chatter, and I chimed in when appropriate. We settled into my room—at least I was getting some use out of the place—and spread the food out on the desk. The longer they talked, the more I managed to pull myself into some semblance of normalcy. My mood lifted, and I was able to silence the chanting voice in the back of my mind insisting I missed the guys.

I watched Jackson, Carter, and Zoe while we ate and bantered. The way they interacted with each other looked so natural. No one scowled when the other two shared a touch. They all looked equally comfortable with little things like a hand-squeeze, a kiss on the cheek, or even a pat on the ass. A tinge of envy wormed through me, not because Jackson had a gorgeous boyfriend—that was always the cause for it in the past—but because they all looked like they wanted to be with each other.

I wasn't greedy. I'd take this from just one person. My chest squeezed in protest, and I ignored it. I never should have let myself project this desire on two strangers, especially convincing myself I clicked with them. My heart hammered harder, almost painfully, against my ribs. Stupid emotions.

"Can I ask you something?" I wasn't sure who I

was talking to, or even why I blurted out the question.

"Always," Jackson said.

"Do you guys ever worry about…?" I clamped my jaw shut when I realized what I was about to say? Why would I do that? I already knew the answer. "Never mind."

"About what?" Zoe asked.

I was happy when Jackson started dating her. She gave him a calm center he hadn't had before. Grounded him, without restricting him. He said she helped him become more… *him*. I never understood what he meant, but maybe I got it more than I admitted. "About what people say. Not about the three of you together. Well, not quite." I wasn't asking this the right way. The words were botched before I even said them. They were all so unique, and didn't seem to care if people saw it, when I felt as if the world watched and judged me the entire time I put myself out there yesterday.

"Are you going to tell me what's going on?" Jackson asked.

"Probably not. Not today, anyway." I wanted to talk about it, but I needed to sort through it first. It had to make more sense to me, before I got someone else's input.

He shrugged. "The thing is people always talk, no matter what you do. They don't limit their whispers to the outgoing girls in their cosplay, or the group of three who can't keep their hands off each other. You can stay single, and they'll gossip. Date a rich guy, a poor guy, a girl, an older man, a younger man—*they'll* have an opinion. Even if you keep your head down and never talk to anyone you think doesn't want to be talked to, someone will have something to say about it." He almost stared right through me, his gaze peering into my soul. "The people who talk will always find something to talk about. That's why you have to ask yourself what you want, instead of what you don't want them to say."

He made it sound so simple. Jackson had told me things like that before, but they never really made sense. They almost did now. Except he still didn't tell me what to do about Evan and Trevor. Let them go—like a normal, sane person would do after twenty-four hours of insane fun and meaningless sex—or listen to the part of me whispering maybe it wasn't so meaningless.

I pushed the rest of my food aside, as my mouthful of orange chicken turned to sawdust. Why couldn't I let this go?

My mood lifted the longer I hung out with my friends. We stayed up way too late, ate too much junk food, watched too many cartoons, and drank more alcohol than I normally consumed in a month. I finally invited them to crash in my hotel room, rather than send them home in a cab.

The next morning, while the pile of three slept soundly on the second bed, I dressed quietly, and made my way downstairs. I'd go pick up breakfast or something. It was the last day of the con; we should make sure we had fun. The problem was, alone with my thoughts and sober, I had time to remember the day before. Longing surged back, and I grabbed my phone. Too bad I didn't have an email address or phone number for Trevor and Evan, but I had their user names.

I shouldn't do this. Trevor's words about regretting speaking up echoed in my head, but I didn't think he believed them any more than I trusted myself. If I didn't do this, I'd never stop wondering what could have been. It wasn't as if I expected either of them to fall down on one knee and confess their undying love, but I did want to spend more time with both of them and see what came next.

I dashed off a quick private message, copying Evan and Trevor on the same note. *I'd like to see you again.*

I didn't want them to believe I was trying to pull them apart. The thought seemed to spring from nowhere—a truth I hadn't recognized yet. It was unreasonable to expect an answer right away, or even at all, but that didn't stop sadness from sinking in when my phone stayed silent. I jumped when it chimed in my hand, then laughed at my own reaction. The text was from Jackson, and my disappointment grew. *Making plans for the day. You anywhere interesting?*

Grabbing breakfast. Back soon, I replied.

I should do that. The hotel had a coffee shop with bagels and muffins. I'd snag us some food there, and head back upstairs. My feet stuck to the floor, legs refusing to move, when I realized Evan stood a few feet away, at the checkout desk. In the second it took him to turn in my direction, a billion options presented themselves to me, boiling down to a smile and acting as if seeing him was nothing, ignoring him and walking away, or telling him at least a little of what was on my mind. The last option terrified me, but it was the only one I could choose.

"Kitten." The nickname sliced into my soul, sharper than any blade. His smile didn't quite form. "I'm sorry I didn't answer your message. I wasn't sure it was a good idea."

"Leaving already?" That was weak. And really obvious. The gears of my mind refused to turn, though.

"Should have left yesterday." He stepped closer, moving out of people's way. His familiar scent, sharp and clean, threatened my grasp on composure. How could I have such a strong reaction to someone I barely knew? He raised a hand, as if to reach for me, then let it drop limply back by his side. "I don't know what Trevor told you."

"Nothing. Not really. That he had to leave early for work, and goodbye."

Evan's laugh was clipped. "Sounds like him. You deserve a little more." His shoulders rose and fell when he sucked in a deep breath and then exhaled. "Look, I know we told you we've done this before, but you were different."

I tried not to read too much into the words, but they already buoyed hope inside. "I feel the same about both of you. I mean that you're different. You already know this was new for me."

His expression wilted. "That's part of the problem. We know this doesn't go past this hotel." He furrowed his brow. "It won't. It can't."

And like that, my mood shattered. I swallowed hard, but couldn't rid myself of the lump in my throat. "Of course."

"The thing is"—he clenched and unclenched his fist—"if you tell yourself it's because this was never meant to be more, if you believe our original intentions are the only reason it's ending, you're doing yourself and the memory a disservice. If you'd prefer, it's not you. It's us. Trevor has been my best friend forever. So long, I barely remember how we met. I like you. I can't speak for him, but it's a fair bet he feels the same. And maybe one of us would click with you, and maybe the other would be happy being a third wheel, or maybe we'd date and it wouldn't work out, and all this over-analyzing would be for nothing. Lots of maybes."

I struggled to process his words without letting my frustration show. My voice wouldn't work, and unshed tears stung my eyes.

"The only *not-maybe,* the only sure thing, is I can't lose Trevor. I'm sorry, Kitten. That's what it comes down to."

They fought over me. It made sense the moment I thought it. I'd known it in the back of my mind, but the same part of me that locked the realization away still denied it was possible, despite the proof I just heard. I forced myself to sound something other than completely bummed out. "I get it. It's okay." It wasn't. Not really. But I didn't want to come between them. "See you around." I stepped back. "Or not. You know.

Whatever." I spun and ducked my head, ignoring anything else Evan had to say. I kept my pace normal as I walked back toward the elevator, despite the prickle in my throat and the burn in my eyes. Why did this hurt so much?

I WAS NEVER ONE OF THOSE PEOPLE WHO HATED Mondays. Work paid the bills, and I didn't mind my job. But two weeks after the convention, my third Monday back in the office, I sat at my desk, staring at my call stats and waiting for the next person to ring through. I wanted to be anywhere else. Or maybe I simply wanted to be at the one place I couldn't. I refused to let myself think their names.

At least I was second-tier support, so I only had to answer questions from other technicians. And we supported networking hardware for large corporations, so most of the people calling in were experienced and professional. I might not be as patient as needed with end-users. I'd already snapped at one tech, when he asked me the same question he called with every other day.

My phone rang, and I forced the cheer into my voice. "Help desk. This is Kathryn. What's up?" We were supposed to use a more formal greeting but had a little leeway for internal people.

"I have a customer asking for a supervisor."

Escalation. *Yay.* My gut twisted in on itself. We

were the next line of support when someone was pissed off and wanted to talk to someone in charge. I guess it kept management free to do their other work. I didn't like talking to pissed-off customers, and they didn't make it to my line unless they were just that. I always cowered and caved the moment they started to yell. "What's the issue?"

"He won't tell me. He demanded a supervisor the moment I picked up, and that's all he'll say."

Ooh, he was extra angry. Even better. I stashed the sarcastic thoughts, swallowed my pending anxiety, and said, "Pass him through." The line clicked, indicating I'd been connected to the caller. "This is Kathryn. I understand you're having an issue. How can I help you today?"

"Hello?"

I refused to roll my eyes. It would crack the shell I had to wrap myself in, to deal with these calls. If I were more like the woman I'd pretended to be at the convention, maybe I'd handle them better. As it was, I already knew I'd bend, break, and acquiesce before the call was over. I always did. "Yes, sir. Hello. How can I help you?"

"I asked to be passed to a supervisor, not a secretary. Let me talk to someone in management."

I clenched my jaw. I could do this. It wouldn't be a problem. I'd take care of things and then go on break, to unwind. "I'm a supervisor. What seems to be the issue?"

"You're not listening, missy." Condescension

oozed from his words. "I want to talk to someone who has the authority to help me, not the gal who answers their phones. Get me someone competent on the line, or I'll have my lawyer contact you."

A growl rose in my chest. I breathed through my nose, focusing on staying calm. "I assure you, I'm able to resolve any issue you're having. Is this a router problem? If you'll give me your company name, I can pull up your hardware information."

"Listen, little lady. I'm trying to be polite, but you're testing my patience. If you don't transfer me now to someone who can help, instead of prattling on in what I'm sure someone thought was a soothing voice, I'm going to start yelling."

Something inside me snapped so cleanly, I swore I felt the rush through me. "Do you have children, sir? A daughter perhaps."

"Not that it's any of your business, but yes. Are you going to transfer me or not?"

My messenger window on my computer chimed with a note from my boss. I ignored it. "What would you do if someone talked to her this way?" I asked. I'd never acted like this at work. It was always suck it up, listen to the shouting, and then apologize until the customer was happy.

"They wouldn't, because my daughter isn't an impertinent bitch."

My blood pressure soared. I muted my computer to keep it from chiming. I was in so much trouble, and I wasn't sure I cared. What happened to me? "Perhaps if she had a father who wasn't a sexist asshole, she'd be a more useful member of society." That wasn't fair; I didn't even know the poor girl. I did pity her, though.

"Listen, you stupid cunt. Do you have any idea who I am?"

My anxiety was gone, replaced with fury. "I don't. Do you know why? Because you haven't given me your fu—"

"I'm sorry about that, sir." A new voice cut into the line, talking over me. Seconds later, my line disconnected. I clenched my teeth, seething with fury.

"Greggers." My barked last name filled the call-center floor. I spun in my chair, to see my boss, Brad, standing in his office door, face red. "In here. Now."

I flung my headset aside and stalked toward him. If every eye in the room hadn't been on me before, they were now. Good. Let them stare and whisper.

Brad shut the door the moment I was inside. "Sit down." His words were clipped. He didn't do the same, standing near his desk instead. "What the hell was that? Quality assurance was on that call, you know."

"Too bad." I shouldn't snap at Brad, but the guy on the phone had me that furious. "If they'd given me thirty more seconds, I would have told that asshole where to stick it."

Brad raised his eyebrows and pursed his lips. "This isn't like you."

"Do you blame me?"

"I can't let you talk like that to customers."

"That's not what I asked." My rage was ebbing, but I still didn't feel I was in the wrong.

He gave a snorting laugh. "I don't blame you, but I still have to write you up."

"Not fire me?" I needed my job. At least until someone came up with a way for me to do anything I wanted without having to pay bills.

"You're good at what you do. Take the rest of the day off. When you come back tomorrow, don't let it happen again."

Except part of me wanted to let it happen again. It felt good to tell that guy what I thought. Even more, I'd rather not come back at all. I wanted to be doing something else. With someone else. Or rather, two someone elses. I couldn't afford to think like that, and I couldn't take any more time to straighten out my head. Real life wouldn't wait while I did.

12

Most of a day off work, completely unplanned. I should be thrilled, regardless of the circumstances. Instead, I found myself sitting in my apartment, staring at the TV without really processing what was on. Now I'd stepped away from the situation at work, I could look at it objectively. What had I been thinking? Yelling at a customer, making things personal…

Except he'd started it. As childish as that sounded in my own mind, it was the best description of the situation. I shouldn't have to roll over and play nice, just because some douche nozzle had wife issues. I expected a surge of nausea at the self-justification. A physical reminder I wasn't allowed to think that way. A ghost of the discomfort was there—an itch that had no source. On the other hand, I felt good about not taking the verbal abuse and speaking up when I needed to.

The con weekend had flipped a switch in my head. Not that I was willing to make myself the life of every party now, but something inside me had changed. Some of my trepidation was gone. The realization brought a sudden wash of sadness with it. A nudge I'd lost something too. Two men I wasn't meant to have.

They'd wanted to end things then and there, but I couldn't let it go. With any luck, now that they'd had time to chill out—that we all had—they'd be more receptive to talking. Who was I kidding? This wasn't a rational decision on my part, the same way yelling at the customer had been completely impulsive. I wanted to see Trevor and Evan again, and I wasn't going to sit around and hope they read my mind from wherever they were.

I sent them a quick DM, copying both of them like I had before. *Thinking of you.* There. Basic enough. Impulse snaked through me, and as an afterthought I also included my phone number.

I didn't have a chance to sink back into the couch before my phone rang. The number on the screen wasn't familiar, and I pressed *Answer* with more enthusiasm than I should have. "Hello?" What I meant to be a cheerful, upbeat greeting came out as tentative.

"Kitten."

A huge weight lifted from me, and I grinned at the empty room. "You called." Not the most brilliant thing I could have said, but I'd done worse.

"I was thinking of you too." Evan's voice calmed the chaos in my head. "I don't like the way we left things at the con."

That made two of us. "Can we meet somewhere? Nothing formal. Coffee or something, all three of us? Take a step back, get to know each other… Just hang out."

His sigh echoed over the line. "I can try, but I have a feeling it'll only be you and me. I'm working late tonight. Tomorrow?"

Was he bummed because Trevor couldn't be there? I had to admit, I didn't like it either, but I still wanted to see Evan. "I have an Aikido class. What if we do it Saturday? I've got all day, and we can figure things out as we go." Did I sound needy? I was okay with that.

"Sounds fantastic." A hesitant note lined his voice.

It wasn't much, but I knew I'd heard it. "I said something wrong."

"No." The cheer was gone from his voice, replaced with something sad. "You said exactly the right thing. In a lot of ways, you remind me of Trevor."

"I'm— Um…" I had no idea how to respond to that. "Thanks?"

He let out a light chuckle. "It's a good thing; I promise. It's just a little bittersweet. He's not talking to me right now."

"Why not?" I asked. A pause carried over the line, and realization clicked in my head. It was because of me. "I'm sorry."

"It's not your fault. I mean that sincerely. I'm not brushing you off." He clucked, as if tossing a thought back and forth. "Anyway. Saturday is perfect."

We figured out a spot we both knew, to meet at, and said our goodbyes. I wanted to say more, but I'd rather it be face to face. I didn't like the idea of having to wait so long to see Evan, but the situation was certainly better than before I messaged him. Maybe it would give me enough time to figure out what I really wanted, instead of getting by on instinct.

I felt like I could breathe again, and still had an entire afternoon free. Nervous energy hummed through me, looking for an outlet. The dojo I worked out at had open classes during the day, where anyone was welcome to participate. It sounded like the perfect solution.

Two and a half hours later, every inch of me ached, and I was in desperate need of a shower, but my mind was clear. I grabbed my phone from my duffel bag, and the flashing light caught my eye. Probably a random email or something. My heart jammed in my throat when I saw the series of text messages, one every thirty minutes or so.

It's Trevor. I got your note.

I'm sure you're busy. Just wanted to say hi.

I don't know why I'm still bugging you.

Probably because I'm thinking of you, too.

I had to stop the giddiness from making my hand shake before I could send back a reply. *I missed you.*

Have dinner with me tomorrow. His answer came seconds later, and I couldn't help but smile.

I have an Aikido class.

Oh.

He didn't give me much to go on, but I wasn't ready for the conversation to be over. I typed back, *Have coffee with us Saturday.*

Us? His message said. *So you're talking to Evan.*

It should have been obvious I reached out to both of them. *He called me back. Was I going to ignore him?*

Busy Saturday. Sorry.

Hurt welled inside. *Fine. Be that way.* It was a childish answer, but he wasn't acting any better.

Wait. If a single word, via text message no less, could convey torrents of meaning, his had. At least I wanted to think that was the case. *I really am busy,* his next message read.

I hovered my fingers over the screen before I typed, *Friday? Just us?*

Seeing them separately wasn't the way to do this, but maybe I could nudge them toward common ground.

I'll be there, he replied.

I needed this to not be a massive mistake.

I headed home, tossing a million ideas around in my head about how to distract myself while I waited for time to pass.

It took about thirty seconds to make sure I updated my phone and associated Evan and Trevor's names with their numbers. Another two minutes, maybe, to put reminders in my calendar for our dates. Not that I needed anything more than my buzzing thoughts to remind me, but it was something to do.

And then I sank onto the couch and stared at the wall. I should watch a movie or something. Or maybe I wanted to go out to eat. This was weird—I never wanted to go out alone. For once, though, I didn't care if people whispered and talked about the girl sitting at a corner table, dining by herself.

I walked back into my apartment around nine. Dinner had been nice, but I wasn't able to stretch it out long enough. Should I watch a movie? Fall asleep early? I wasn't tired.

My phone rang, and I jumped. I laughed at the empty apartment and my own skittishness. A smile threatened to split my face when I saw Evan's name on the screen.

"Hey." Giddiness fluttered in my chest. "I thought you were working."

"I just got off."

"And you didn't let me watch." *Oops, maybe I shouldn't have said that.*

His laugh relaxed me. "You're going to kill me with lines like that." He sounded like he looked forward to it.

I sat down, and pulled a throw pillow onto my lap. "I could apologize if that helps."

"Definitely don't do that. I like knowing you

meant it. Besides, I was thinking it, so I would be disappointed if you didn't say anything."

I wanted to take the flirting further. Fall into the teasing. The excitement racing over my skin made me curious to see how far we could go over the phone. Except, something about getting too sexy with just Evan felt like cheating. It wasn't a rational thought, but that didn't make it any easier for me to feel otherwise. "What's up?" That sounded casual, right?

"Honestly? I just wanted to talk."

"And you called me? I'm flattered." I tried to sound flippant, but the sentiment had me glowing.

"You should be. I didn't want to talk to anyone else…"

Except Trevor. I almost heard the words buried in his unfinished sentence, and I didn't know how to respond.

"I wanted to hear your voice." Evan's tone firmed and took on the confidence I expected from him.

I lost track of time as we fell into conversation, touching on everything from what movies we were waiting for to places we'd love to visit, to how we felt about karma.

When I yawned for the fourth time in as many minutes, he said, "You need your sleep, Kitten."

Was it really almost two? I didn't want to hang up, but we both had work in the morning, and mine promised to be horrible even without exhaustion looming over me. "Sleep is for the weak."

"Then that's me." His voice took on a somber tone. "I'll see you this weekend."

We said reluctant goodbyes, and I barely remembered to strip out of my clothes before collapsing in bed.

Waking up Tuesday morning was like grating my soul over a gravel pit. I forced myself to follow my routine. Go to work. Ignore the stares. Not yell at obnoxious customers. Head to the dojo.

I was dragging by the time I made it home that night. I needed to unwind after my workout, and a shower helped, but experience told me my muscles would hate me in the morning if I didn't sit up for at least a little while.

I settled on the couch and grabbed the remote. My phone buzzed with a new text. A second wind of energy rushed through me when I saw a message from Trevor.

What're you up to? he asked.

Deciding what to watch.

Oh :(

His frowny face drew a similar expression from

me. How was I supposed to interpret it? *I should be staring at the wall instead?* I hoped he'd get the teasing in my response.

No. I just wanted to catch you after class and before your shower.

I adored that he'd messaged me, but unlike with to Evan, over the phone, I struggled to infer the tone of the conversation based on typed words. *Because…?*

To give you something to fantasize about, while you rinsed off.

Oh. Heat flooded my skin, and any doubt about his tone evaporated. *You're assuming I wasn't already thinking about it.* If I hadn't been before, I was now. Slipping and sliding together in the shower. My pulse raced at the vivid images.

His reply made my phone vibrate in my hand. *Me stepping up behind you? Wrapping my arms around your waist. Both of us soapy and wet…*

Fuck. That whole *this feels like cheating* thing was back, looming at the forefront of my thoughts. I didn't know what to say.

Except in your version, there are more than two of us.

I almost heard his disappointment. *I'd apologize, but I'm not sorry,* I sent back. No reason to keep avoiding this. I knew what I wanted. The revelation startled me. I really did know what I wanted, and it was both of them. Without a doubt. *It's not the same if you're not both there.*

Nothing. Several minutes passed without a reply. Had my message gone through? Had I pissed him off? I fumbled with a follow-up text, fluctuating between teasing and serious.

His response buzzed in first. *So, what are we watching?*

I didn't want to leave things like that, brushing over my comment as if it never existed, but this wasn't the medium to have the conversation in. I'd see him face to face on Friday.

I should send back a series name. We'd be ridiculous and watch the same thing at the same time.

Damn it, I couldn't leave things this way. *I'm serious.*

Would things have been different if we met without Evan? Trevor's question burrowed deep into my thoughts. Shock hit me first. I shouldn't be surprised he asked, but it still felt like icy water racing down my spine. The longer the words lingered in my head, the more they hurt. *Would you really take that from me? From us?*

If you already know he's what you want, why are we talking? You've made up your mind. Why lead me on?

I clenched my jaw at the accusation, especially since I'd just told him this wasn't what I wanted. *You're misinterpreting my words. Fuck that. You're just being an ass.*

Spell it out for me, so I don't have to guess.

Were we really fighting via text message? One of the guys I wasn't actually dating, who I was never supposed to see again after two weeks ago? It was ludicrous and infuriating, and it felt right. *I already spelled it out. More than once. Don't make me choose.*

I'm sorry. I'm being cruel.

Damn straight. Instead of sending back my gut response, I typed, *I don't know what else to do but be honest with you. I don't want this to be you versus Evan. I don't know why you think it has to be.*

Because that's how relationships work. Two people hook up, form a bond, and see how far they want to take things…

No, I typed. *That's how most relationships work. If we want something different, we can make up our own rules.*

Just because you know someone who made it happen, doesn't mean it's that easy or that everyone can do it.

He was being stubborn. I growled at the empty room and forced myself to think rationally. *I'm not saying everyone can do it. I'm suggesting in our case…*

Big difference here, Kathryn. Your brother likes guys and girls. I've only got the one preference. It's not like I can just flip a switch because you think it sounds like a good idea.

I didn't have an argument for that. *I know. I was just hoping…* What? Trevor was right.

Hoping it would be different with Evan? He's still got the wrong body parts.

But he's your best friend. Wow, that was weak. I hated to admit defeat, but I couldn't force either of them into this if they didn't want it.

Just because I hang out with the guy doesn't mean I want him sucking me off.

You're right. I'm sorry.

Me too.

Was the conversation over? Did he expect me to say something else? He hadn't given me a lot to go on. Several minutes passed without another response. Maybe I ruined any chance we had at finding common ground. Not that there ever had a chance, based on our exchange.

A note buzzed through. *What are we watching?*

I should tell him nothing, and that I needed to go, but I wasn't ready to end things like that. *Something classic. High action. And really corny.*

Captain Harlock?

Maybe if we couldn't have a romantic relationship, we could have a friendship. I sent back, *Sounds great.*

We spent the next couple hours exchanging quips about how good or bad or just plain funny the movie was.

14

Wednesday came and went without contact from Evan or Trevor, and I couldn't ignore my disappointment, even if it was unreasonable. On Thursday, I decided it was ridiculous to wait for them, and sent them both a *good morning :)* Trevor replied with a similar message, but it hurt when I didn't hear from Evan.

Thursday afternoon, I finished up Aikido class, shouldered my duffel bag, and hovered at the edge of the floor mats, watching the next class. They guy teaching was a classmate of mine. He'd been doing this for years, like I had, and now he stood up there, in front of a group of pre-teens, taking them through their forms.

I wanted to be doing that. Why wasn't I? I had no right wishing Evan and Trevor would step up and recognize how they felt, if I wasn't willing to do the same. I was happy to admit how I felt about them, but

I was still holding back when it came to work. I set my bag aside and padded to the main office.

My sensei—the guy who owned the dojo—looked up from his computer. "What's up?"

I twisted my fingers in on themselves, grabbed my will to do this from deep inside, and stood straighter. "I'd like another chance teaching."

He shook his head and turned back to whatever he was working on. "I'm sorry, Kathryn. You're very talented. It's obvious you love doing this, and you've learned a lot over the years. But you don't have the kind of presence a teacher needs."

The words stung even more the second time around, and left my skin prickling. I shoved it aside and forced the confidence into my voice. "I don't agree. I think I can do this."

Now I had his full attention. His brows were half raised, his eyes wide. A combination of surprise and... hope? "You did poorly during your practical test," he said.

That was the part where I had to actually teach a class. "I know. It was a poor performance. I really think I can do better. Let me assist someone else, to prove it. Then if I do better, let me take on classes of my own?"

He drummed his fingers on his keyboard, not compressing any keys, and then stood. "All right. One more chance. Do this, and I'll let you start teaching classes. Follow me."

I fell into step behind him but almost stopped

moving when he stepped up in front of the current class. He halted them and bowed. A dozen heads returned the polite gesture. "We have a special treat today," he told them. "One of our black belts, Kathryn, is going to face off with your sensei. It will give you an idea of what you'll be able to do if you keep at this."

All those faces turned in my direction, and a hot flush spread over my face. I gritted my teeth, locked my hesitation aside and stepped to the front of the class. I could do this; that was the point. What Jackson had told me bounced in my head. It didn't matter how many people watched. Those who were going to talk would do so, no matter what. Besides, these kids were living life, like the rest of us.

I bowed to my counterpart, and we both fell into defensive stances. A twitch from his foot, and the spar began.

For the next five minutes, to the tune of gasps, claps, and *oohs*, we grappled, tumbled, and danced. The demonstration ended with me dropping him to the mat and pinning him until he tapped out. I helped him to his feet, we faced the class, and gave one more bow. Seconds later, the kids surrounded us, asking questions and talking over each other. They looked at me in awe, instead of disgust or amusement.

Sensei stood at the far end of the mats. He gave me a small smile. "One week. You help with classes. Then we'll see. Email me your schedule, and I'll fit you in."

I wanted to squeal and clap and give him a thank-you hug, but I restrained myself. Instead I simply bowed. "You'll have my schedule tonight. Thank you."

My mood increased another notch when I pulled my phone out on the way to my car. One missed call, from Evan. I dialed my voicemail and dropped into my vehicle.

"Hey, Kitten." His voice was more soothing that I thought possible. "I've been in meetings with contractors on the East Coast since early this morning, and just got your note. If you're free, call me."

I wanted to get him on the line right away, but I also wanted to be somewhere I wouldn't have to hang up anytime soon. Traffic seemed to flow like molasses as I drove home. By the time I unlocked my apartment door and pushed inside, every inch of me was tense. I tossed my duffle bag aside, already bringing up Evan's number.

"I think I'm addicted to your voice," he said as a greeting. "I'd much rather hear you say *good morning* than see a text. Not that I'm complaining."

Even though it had been almost two days, the conversation with Trevor was still fresh in my mind. Not that I'd re-read the messages or anything, trying to figure if I could have said something different. Well, not more than a few times. Would flirting with Evan end in the same disaster? I couldn't be rude. "How about a *good evening*, instead?"

"It's a start." His smile was audible. "At least one of you is still talking to me."

That answered the question of whether or not bringing up Trevor was off the table. "I'm sorry you haven't heard from him." Was this my segue to ask if Evan was interested in a more-than-two-person relationship? I didn't have any right. Trevor made himself clear, so even if Evan was interested in the same thing as I was, it wasn't going to happen.

"Can I tell you something?" Evan asked. His voice was so quiet, I had to strain to hear him.

A million possibilities raced through my head. Among them, the selfish option that he'd spend more time with me regardless. But I'd struggle with only being with one of them. I needed to stop guessing, before I drove myself insane. "Of course."

"For the longest time, I thought I was gay."

Wow, that came out of nowhere. And here I thought *I* was about to dump an intense conversation on us. "Past tense?"

"Trevor doesn't know. It's the one thing I never told him, growing up. Because"—Evan sighed—"he was the reason I thought that, and there was no way I'd tell my best friend I was interested in him *like that.*"

The air rushed from my lungs, as if a vice squeezed them tight. That was nowhere on my list of guesses. Should I feel bad that it was a relief to hear it? "What did you do?"

"When we hit high school, I got so much tail, it distracted me. Football team, student council… It was easy. I threw myself into being with girls, and it wasn't bad. If I pretended hard enough, Trevor was just another guy. I don't know why I'm dumping this on you. Like I said, you remind me of him, but you're different."

"It's okay. I don't mind." I was intensely curious, but it was only my business if he felt like sharing. It didn't feel right to push.

"Thanks." A hint of relief lifted his voice. "So I enlisted, thought I'd put it all behind me, and when my bunkmate hit on me, I wasn't into it. There weren't any other guys catching my attention. I came back, and there Trevor was. My best friend and the only guy I dreamed about at night."

"I don't blame you for dreaming about him." I tried to keep my tone light and teasing, but still sympathetic.

"Because you've got good taste." More of the tension faded from his voice. "The first time we picked up a girl together, it was my idea. I needed an excuse, and that felt more subtle than, *I think you're hot, but I need to suck you off to find out if it means anything*. It turned out we both liked the experience, though he didn't enjoy it for the same reasons I did. So now you know my secret. I pick up women with my best friend, as an excuse to be with him. And then you came along and—"

My heart sank. "Got in the way."

"No." He spoke quickly. "Completely the opposite. You fit too well, but he and I don't have *that.*"

"Maybe you could." It was selfish of me to encourage Evan, knowing how Trevor felt, but I couldn't take it back.

"Not going to happen," he said. "I've hinted at it, asked him indirectly, and he's not interested."

"What if the question simply needs to be asked differently?"

"No."

I hadn't expected the abrupt retort. "Okay. Forget it."

"It's not that. I meant it when I said I can't lose him. Dancing around the subject is better than the last few weeks of not talking to him have been."

"I'm having dinner with him tomorrow night." I shouldn't have said that.

"He gets you first?"

Defensiveness raced through me. "It's not like that."

"I know. I didn't mean it to be."

I twisted my ponytail around my finger. "Meet up with us. Talk it out. Not necessarily *that,* but make things right with him." I was negotiating for them, as much as for me. An empty ache grew inside when Evan sighed again. I wanted to see him happy, with or without me.

"I see what you're trying to do, and I appreciate it"—his voice was low and sad—"but this has to stay between you and me. Always. Promise me."

"Of course." I could do nothing else, given the intensity in his plea.

"It's not right that I have to make this choice. In a perfect world, I'd know he felt the same, we'd get to know you better, and... This isn't that world. He's only interested in me as a friend, and neither of us is mature enough to see you with the other. God, Kitten, it kills me things happened this way."

"Me too." Killed me. Devoured me. Tore me apart. "But think about it. Please? I'll send you the address."

"You're meeting at the Italian place on Fourth and Thirteenth, at eight."

I stared my phone for a minute. "Did he...?"

"I assumed he set the time and place. Lucky guess on my part." Evan's words were tinged with sadness. "I'll think about it. If I'm not there though, please don't take it personally."

"How else am I supposed to take it?"

"Good point." His laugh was strained.

We chatted for a while longer, but the levity that was there during the con and on Tuesday was missing. A heavy cloud hung over the conversation, nagging that this wasn't going the way either of us wanted.

When we hung up, I sent Trevor a text. I didn't think anything would come of it, but that didn't stop me from hoping.

I invited Evan to join us tomorrow night.

I couldn't wait for a reply. I sent one message after another. *I don't know if he'll show.*

And if you don't either, I'll understand.

It'll hurt, but I'll understand.

But you can't let this ruin your friendship. The two of you deserve more than that. So let him make things better between you. I had no intention of breaking my promise to Evan. I was willing to take a lot more of a stand than I used to, when it came to anything, but I couldn't try to open Trevor's eyes when this wasn't my secret to share.

I could push and prod for them to work things out, though.

I SAT IN THE RESTAURANT PARKING LOT, STARING AT MY steering wheel and listening to my mind ramble on. I wanted to walk in there and tell Trevor how it was. Nudge him until he admitted he felt the same way about Evan and me that we did about him. Except that wasn't my right. I'd already told him how I felt, but the rest was out of my hands.

The clock ticked up on meeting time, and I stashed my internal argument. Maybe it was time to play things by ear. I found Trevor on the sidewalk, right outside the front door, his hands jammed in his pockets. He grinned when he saw me, and my heart danced happily against my ribs. I reached out for a tentative hug. He squeezed me tight, and I sank into the embrace. I hadn't realized how much I missed this the last couple of weeks. Part of me wanted more. A kiss, long and passionate.

"I missed you," he murmured against my hair. "And I'm sorry for how I left things the other night." His apology sank into me, soothing an anxiety I hadn't been able to quell.

"I thought you might not show, because of the messages I sent last night." I didn't want to bring them up, but sweeping them under the rug wouldn't help anyone.

"I almost didn't." He pulled back enough to study my face. "I… uh… made a call, after you texted me. What you said on Tuesday made me think about things I've been trying really hard not to think about. I don't know if I can do what you're asking, but you're right. I don't want to lose my best friend."

A hand settled on the small of my back. I assumed not Trevor's, since he still grasped my hips.

"Hey, Kitten." Evan's familiar voice lifted my spirits further. I leaned back into his touch, careful not to break contact with Trevor.

"We talked a lot," Trevor said.

This had to be good news, or they wouldn't both be here. "And…?"

"But not about *everything*," Evan added.

Trevor furrowed his brow. "Apparently there are some things he can't say without you here. You're his translator?"

"I don't think that's quite right." Then again, I didn't know for certain. Evan seemed to hold a few missing pieces to this conversation. I reluctantly extracted myself from his touch and turned to face him. "I can't translate, unless I know what I'm saying."

"Let's go inside." Evan nudged me. "We'll sit. We'll talk."

Trevor trailed his hand down my arm and tangled his fingers with mine. "Come on."

Whatever they'd hashed out, apparently the jealousy had faded. Neither one of them seemed to have a problem with the other touching me. I wasn't complaining, but I wondered what I'd missed.

I stepped away and leaned against the wall, so I could see them both. "I won't be tag-teamed." I winced as soon as the words were out of my mouth. Maybe not the best phrasing.

Evan lowered his mouth to my ear, his voice quiet. "I thought this was part of the point."

Trevor shook his head, but he didn't look irritated. "Inside. We'll talk. Or someone will." He shot Evan a pointed glare.

"Fine." Evan held his hands up in surrender, but he was smiling.

Moments later, we were seated at a in the back of the restaurant. Evan and Trevor knew the host, so despite the Friday night crowd, we had a premium, almost private spot. I hesitated next to the booth. Who sat next to whom?

Each guy slid into a separate side, making my decision even more difficult. Trevor grabbed my hand

and tugged, and Evan didn't look even a little bit hurt by the gesture. This was too easy.

I locked my gaze on Evan. "What did you tell him?"

Evan stared back without hesitation. "I told him I'd back down if you both wanted me to, but he had to hear me out, and you had to be okay with it."

I pursed my lips and looked between the two. "I think I've made myself clear."

Trevor squeezed my knee. I wanted to be irritated with him— with both of them—for spoon-feeding me this information, but the gesture was reassuring. He opened and closed his mouth a few times, before finally speaking. "I told him I wasn't going to choose between him and you."

Great. Now we were back to the part where Kathryn stepped aside, so two great guys could stay friends. I didn't begrudge them the decision, but I would miss them. A lump grew in my throat, and I tried to swallow past it. "And?"

"And he got really stubborn and just kept repeating I had to hear him out and you had to be there."

I looked back at Evan. "Are you enjoying this?"

His smugness faltered. "Not as much as you might think. I'm kind of terrified, honestly. I know what I said before, but maybe you could—"

"No." I kept my voice kind. As much as I wanted this out in the open, it wasn't my place to do the revealing.

Evan waved down the waiter and ordered three beers. He shifted in his seat, and then again, before he finally looked at Trevor. "I love you." The words ran together in a single syllable.

I almost didn't want to look at Trevor, but I had to know. His expression was blank, except for his wide eyes. I swore I heard a clock somewhere, ticking away the seconds as silence stretched across the table.

"You mean her, right?" Trevor's question came out strained.

Evan frowned. "Soon, probably. Though, no offense Kitten, we're not there yet. I mean you, Trevor. My best friend. The guy who's always been there. The only man I've ever dreamed about, and they're some intense fucking dreams."

"I can't—" Trevor nudged me.

I slid out of his way, and he brushed past me without another word, to vanish out the front door seconds later.

"That went well." Evan grabbed one of the beers the waiter set on the table and drained half the bottle in a single swallow.

"Give him a little time to process?" I wasn't sure what I was saying. They knew each other better than I did. Now even more than before.

Evan scrubbed his face. "What if time doesn't fix it?"

I gave him what I hoped was a reassuring smile. "It's been thirty seconds. Too soon to tell. Besides, you both showed up tonight, and I think that counts for something."

"I was so glad he called me." Evan slammed the bottle into the table. "I have to go talk to him." He fished a twenty from his wallet and tossed it next to the drinks. He stood and held out his hand.

"You want me to come with you?"

"You're in this with us. I would never say you caused it—don't think that—but meeting you was the catalyst." He pulled me to my feet. "You'd rather I do it without you?"

I fell into step beside him. "No. I just didn't want to assume."

He muttered a quick apology to the host, said something came up, and held the front door open for me.

We found Trevor on the side of the building, back to the wall and one foot propped up. His gaze was directed at the night sky, and he didn't move when we shuffled up next to him. "Give a guy some warning, why don't you?" His voice was quiet.

"I don't have any practice with this kind of thing," Evan said dryly. "Was I supposed to lead with, *I have this friend who likes you…*?"

Trevor pushed from the wall and finally looked at Evan. "It might have helped. Do you want a do-over?"

"Not really. It won't change anything."

Trevor raked shaky fingers through his hair. "In that case, me too."

I almost asked when he meant, but my brain caught up before the question spilled out. He was talking about loving Evan. Hope sparked inside me. I couldn't find the strength to suppress it, but I didn't dare speak and ruin the moment.

"I told you I've been thinking a lot over the past couple of weeks"—Trevor took another step toward Evan, gravel lining his voice—"and not just about Kathryn, though God damn if that woman isn't addictive." He kept his gaze on Evan, but his words sent another flutter through me. "She's not the reason I couldn't call you. I'd be pissed if the two of you hooked up without me, though."

Evan opened his mouth, and Trevor held up a warning finger. "I'm not done." His gaze never left Evan. "It was really easy to ignore how I felt, once you enlisted, but then you came back. Don't get me wrong; I've never been more grateful for something. Then you had to suggest we pick up a girl together. And fuck if I wasn't willing to do it again and again, just to be with you. Not that I could admit to myself that's why I did it. It didn't matter how many times I woke up in the middle of the night, cock hard as a rock, your image burned in my dreams, driving me to beat off until I was raw. I still wasn't interested in you. That's what I told myself."

The intensity in Trevor's confession stole my breath and sent my imagination running rampant. It filled me with a rainbow of conflicting and complimentary emotions. I didn't know if I was relieved, worried I was about to lose them both, or happy to see them finally admitting the truth.

Trevor stopped with his shoes nudging Evan's. While a mixture of hope and concern peppered Evan's face, Trevor didn't reflect any emotion. His voice was heavy. "And then she came along, and the two of you were good together. Incredible, even. And something pinged in the back of my mind that I was about to lose her. Which made no sense, because I didn't have her. When you stormed out of our hotel room that morning because she was wearing my shirt, I was terrified. More scared than I'd been since they deployed you to a fucking war zone. Because I have to have you in my life."

Trevor tangled his fingers in Evan's hair and kissed him hard, mouths crushing together, moans mingling. If being pressed between the two of them was hot, this was scorching. A bitter copper taste hit my tongue, and I realized I was biting my lip.

"So are we good?" Evan was breathless when they broke apart.

"I fucking hope so." Trevor finally looked at me. "You're really tough on a guy's psyche. You know that? Making me think, and admit I have feelings, and all that bullshit?"

I laughed, as much to let the tension out as anything. "I didn't mean to."

"That's part of what makes you so amazing." He wove his fingers with mine, other hand still settled on the back of Evan's neck. "You're just making it up as you go along."

I couldn't hide my grin. "So do we all want the same thing? No having to choose. No pitting you against each other?"

"I'm in." Trevor squeezed my hand.

Evan spun me to face him and brushed his lips over mine. "Me too." He kissed me again, more deeply this time. He slid his tongue into my mouth and it danced around mine. Heat and hunger made my blood roar, and my need grew, drawing my nipples to hard nubs and pooling wet between my thighs.

Trevor tightened his grip on my hand and sucked in a deep breath through his teeth. His response heightened my arousal. "I'm thinking it's a good thing we brought this outside." His voice was strained.

"My place is about five minutes away." Evan nodded toward the main road. "We could talk about this in a more intimate setting."

The way he said *intimate* sent a pleasant shiver through me. "Yes, please," I said.

"Wait." Trevor tugged me back. "Is it really this easy?"

Disappointment set in at the hesitation, but it didn't ease my arousal. "You call two weeks—or several years in your cases—of soul searching and denial *easy*?"

Trevor studied my face, as if he might find some deep, mysterious answer hidden there. "Why did you push this? You and I click. It's like we operate on the same wavelength sometimes. We're incredible together."

His words both warmed and worried me. I thought he wanted both of us. Except I was too focused on what Trevor said and not on how he said it. This wasn't accusation or regret. His tone was curious.

And he deserved an answer, rather than me making broad statements like, *Now we all belong to each other, 'kay?*

Two gazes lingered on me, heavy with expectation. "Kathryn?"

Playing things by ear. Right. I needed to dive in and hope I didn't say something stupid. "It's true; we do. But I click with Evan too. You just said so. I don't need to justify it. You see as well as I do that the three of us work."

Trevor's mouth twitched in an unformed smile. "So how does this go? Do we always all have to be around?"

I raised my brows. "First of all, I'm talking about more than just sex. It's not like all three of us are always going to be in the same place at the same time. Beyond that, do we have to label it? Sometimes it's going to be all three of us, and sometimes someone will be busy or not in the mood, and I figure it's all okay as long as there are no secrets. We still need to get to know each other and get comfortable with our dynamic. No reason to put a fence around it before we even know what *it* is."

"So"—Evan dragged the word out—"if Trevor and

I were to hook up when you weren't around, you'd be okay with it, as long as someone told you about it after, in vivid, lurid, filthy detail?"

A visual rolled through my thoughts. The two of them stripped down, kissing, hands roaming each other's hard, bare bodies. I squeezed my legs together, to suppress the throb, and chewed my bottom lip. "I'd rather someone took pictures. But I guess if the photographer's busy, a verbal play-by-play would be all right."

Evan prompted me toward the parking lot again, but locked his gaze on Trevor. "*Now* we're going back to my place."

THE DRIVE TO EVAN'S HOUSE MIGHT HAVE BEEN THE longest five minutes of my life. I was squirming by the time he led us inside.

Before the door was all the way closed, Trevor twisted his fingers in my hair and held my head captive. "God, I missed you," he growled before crushing his mouth to mine.

I whimpered at the intensity, the weight of his kiss driving into me.

I dug my fingers into his chest, needing something —anything—to hold onto, and slid my body against his. The faint scent of his body wash, cool and sharp, filled my thoughts and dialed up my pulse another notch.

Evan brushed my hair off the back of my neck, and a second set of lips traced over my skin.. I whimpered against Trevor's mouth. Trevor dropped his other hand to my waist and pushed under my T-shirt. The heat of his palm on my stomach was like a million sparks of energy, flaring across my skin. Evan nipped my earlobe with his teeth and then trailed his tongue down my neck. His erection dug into my ass, hard and insistent. God, I loved being caught between these two. I never imagined it could be like this.

Evan sucked on my sensitive skin. Biting. Flicking his tongue over the flesh. Marking me. Trevor glided his hand higher until he cupped my breast. He kneaded, pressure and focus increasing until he pinched my nipple through the fabric. He rolled the hard nub, sending a delicious spike of pain and pleasure through me. I needed to be closer. To feel more. I grabbed the hem of Trevor's shirt. He broke the contact long enough to yank the Tee over his head and toss it aside.

Evan continued his attentions along my shoulder, hands on my hips and fingers gripping tight. His every groan vibrated through his chest and my back. I worked my pelvis in rhythm, grinding against the shaft digging into me.

I traced Trevor's slender torso, following the lines and definition. I dragged a thumb over his nipple. He sucked in a sharp breath when I drew tight circles around the button. He looked me over, lust darkening his gaze. "You've got too many clothes on."

"I agree." Evan stripped my shirt off in a single, fluid gesture. I barely registered lifting my arms long enough for him to do so. Trevor shoved my bra up, building friction and scraping skin in need of more attention. He lowered his mouth and flicked his tongue over my swollen nipple. I gasped at the light gesture and the shock of cool, when he blew on the skin.

The tension on my shoulders vanished when Evan unsnapped my bra and drew it away. Trevor took my nipple in his mouth, and sucked. He massaged my other breast, pinching and tugging in time with his mouth. I shifted my weight. My lower lips slid easily, already wet in anticipation. Evan grabbed my hips again and pulled me back into his cock. The hard shaft teased me through denim, and he grunted every time I pressed back.

I scraped a nail down Trevor's chest, past the waistband of his jeans and to the thick bulge waiting for attention. He jerked against my touch and sucked my nipple harder. There were too many sensations, and at the same time not enough contact. Their scents mingled and filled my head, and their voices were the most erotic song I'd ever heard.

I stroked Trevor through his pants, pumping my hips with each new touch, bite, or squeeze from either man.

"I bet you're soaked, Kitten." Evan's voice had dropped an octave.

"You'll never know unless you check." It took

more focus than I wanted, to keep the teasing in my voice amid the rainbow of sensations driving over me.

Evan sought out my button and zipper. Seconds later, he dragged the remainder of my clothing down my legs. Searing heat built over my skin, and the air kissed my wet mound. His fingers pushed between my legs from behind, parting my folds.

"This is amazing." I forced the words out between gasps and locked my gaze on Trevor. "But I want something else."

He smirked and pulled his mouth from my breast, hand still kneading. Evan's touch danced along my slit, light enough to tease, never making contact with my clit or dipping inside me.

Trevor studied my face, green eyes wide and curious. "Anything you want."

"You." I nudged his shoulders, guiding him back toward the sofa. "I want to taste you." I fumbled with his belt and jeans for only a moment, before undoing both and pushing those plus his boxer briefs to the ground.

He landed on the couch with a quiet grunt, his cock at full mast, begging for attention.

I knelt next to him, wrapped my hand around the base, and stroked. "This time, let me finish you?" I held his gaze, my voice gravelly with desire.

"Fuck, yes." Evan's words melded with the moment.

Trevor traced a finger over my bottom lip, pulling

it into a pout before letting go. His smile grew. "How am I going to say *no* to a request like that?"

I dipped my head but kept my gaze on Trevor's, as I flicked my tongue over the tip of his cock. He groaned and dug his fingers into my shoulder. The sharp pressure spurred me on. I took his entire length in my mouth. Evan dipped between my pussy lips again, still tracing over skin and teasing. My head swam from so much sensory input, feeling light, as if it might float away at any minute. The room buzzed with gasps and groans. I knew exactly which belonged to whom, but they still mingled in an intoxicating melody.

I stroked Trevor's shaft while I sucked, speeding up according to the sounds he made. Evan slid a finger inside me, and I groaned in delight. My clit ached for attention, throbbing more each second I ministered to Trevor. I shifted my hand to cup his balls, which were already tight. He rested a hand at the back of my neck, holding me in place and guiding the pace. I was trapped between the two of them, hovering near the height of pleasure, held in place by hands and unseen bonds. My heart screamed in excitement.

Trevor's hand tightened, and his breathing grew punctuated. "God, Kathryn, I'm gonna come."

His words almost had the same effect on me, especially with Evan's finger gliding in and out of me at a slow, steady pace. I sucked Trevor hungrily, bobbing against him. He rose off the couch with a loud moan, and warm, salty fluid hit the back of my throat. I continued to lick and stroke until he shuddered away from my touch.

As I pulled back, my satisfied grin vanished in a moan when Evan shoved more fingers inside me, enough to stretch me out. Trevor grasped my face, and pulled me up to kiss me, tasting himself on my lips, thrusting his tongue into my mouth, and swallowing my cries.

I was vaguely aware of the sound of a zipper behind me. Evan pumped his hand against my opening.

Trevor dipped his head next to my ear. "I wanna see you come. Hard." His lips moved against my skin, his words as much touch as whisper. "I wanna see Evan bury his thick dick inside you, all the way to the hilt, and I want to hear you scream in pleasure."

It took the last of my resources to summon a response. "That's a long list."

Trevor nibbled on my ear. "And you're not

complaining." He slid two fingers down my breastbone, over my stomach, and between my legs, and found my clit with little searching.

The new touch, abrading my already swollen sex, mingled with the sensation of the fingers hooked inside me and hitting just the right spot. Orgasm shredded through me, flooding my limbs and leaving me wobbly. My body jerked from Trevor's touch when my clit protested at the over-stimulation, but he kept up the pressure. Evan pulled his fingers out of me, but seconds later a blunt head nudged my opening.

Evan drove his cock deep inside me and grabbed my hips tight, slamming his pelvis against my butt. "You're so tight, Kitten." It sounded as if he spoke through clenched teeth.

I couldn't muster a response. The two contrasting and complimentary touches had me hovering near climax again, but my body refused to yield. Evan tightened his grip, and his breathing grew shallow. The short strokes from behind and gasps for air made me think he was as close as I was.

With his free hand, Trevor sought out my nipple again. He resumed the attention he'd given it moments ago, but this time the rough pinch met already tender skin. The new spark sent me over the edge. I screamed when I came. Stars danced in my vision, as arcs of pleasure and release spilled through me. My pussy clenched around Evan's dick. Spasming. Gripping.

Trevor eased back in time with my slowing gasps.

Evan let out a series of short grunts followed by a long groan, and I knew he'd finished as well.

Euphoria sank in, as the room spun to a stop and my surroundings blurred back into focus. My head still buzzed from the overload, and a giddy laugh escaped my throat. My legs wobbled, and from Evan's faltering grip behind me, I wondered if he felt the same. Trevor helped me shift and drew me into his lap. Evan dropped onto the couch next to us. He pulled my legs over his and leaned his head on Trevor's shoulder.

The only sound in the room was breathing returning to normal. A few short weeks ago, I'd never have guessed this could be me. But now, wrapped into a pleasant tangle with two wonderful men, I couldn't imagine things happening any other way. Trevor rested his head on Evan's and traced tiny circles over my shoulder blade. Evan covered my shins with his palms.

Yup. This was absolutely perfect.

THREE MONTHS LATER

I glanced one last time at the king-size bed in my hotel room, grateful someone else was paid to make the bed this weekend, and let the door swing shut behind me. I strode toward the elevator, skirt swishing around my legs. Back in L.A., for the first time in years. Attending one of the conventions that started my love of these things was exciting. Especially when I was with the two men who inspired so many other new things in me.

I squished into the waiting car, not minding that it was already too full of people. The last few months were an amazing ride of discovery. Getting to know Trevor and Evan better. Falling into my teaching role at the dojo. Handing in my resignation at the call center.

For the first several weeks, Trevor made it a habit to point out things still might not work. We didn't all know each other. The thrill would wear off. Life would intrude. He hadn't brought up any doubts in a while. When I'd asked him about it, he said he'd decided there was no reason to worry.

I didn't know what the odds were my brother and I would both end up in poly relationships, but Jackson was as supportive of the entire thing as he always was—after a few threatening glares and muttered warnings about my guys not breaking his little sister's heart.

The elevator slowed to a stop on the main floor, and people spilled out. I stepped out of the flow of traffic and positioned myself near a blank slice of wall. Where to look for Evan and Trevor first? They both ducked out early this morning, wanting to attend panels that didn't hold the same appeal to me as sleeping in.

A finger trailed down my spine, leaving a delicious tingle in its wake and ending with a palm cupping my ass. "A cute little kitten like you shouldn't be wandering a place like this alone."

I leaned back into Evan with a smile, inhaling his familiar, crisp scent. "I'm not alone if you're here."

"Hmm..." He trailed his lips along the back of my neck. "I don't have an argument for that."

Amusement bubbled inside. This was going to be an awesome weekend. "Were *you* alone?"

"Nope." Trevor stepped up in front of me. I had no idea if he'd magically materialized, or the crowds had parted to let him through. He handed me a cup of coffee. "I thought you'd want this."

I took a long sip of the drink, not caring it scalded going down. "My hero."

Trevor kissed me on the cheek. "Only for you." He paused, raised his brows, and nodded at Evan. "And him, I guess. But I don't fetch coffee for anyone else."

Evan gave my butt a light squeeze. "You know, half the guys here watched you waltz off that elevator."

Months ago, I would have been mortified to hear that. The impulse to be embarrassed was still there, but it was overridden by a hint of pride. "More of them would stare if they knew what I'm—sorry, what I'm not—wearing under my skirt."

Evan inched my skirt up, until his fingers brushed bare skin. A tremor ran through me. It didn't matter how much we experimented or what kind of things we got up to, either one of them still made me wet with a single touch.

"No distracting him." Despite Trevor's words, his gaze drifted below my waist. "For at least a couple of minutes. We were talking this morning, and Evan wants to ask you something."

"The answer's yes, if you can find us a restroom with locking doors down here." I kept my tone light and teasing, imagination already skipping ahead to me being pushed up to the edge of the sink, skirt hiked over my hips—

"Not that." Evan cut into my thoughts. "Well maybe that, but this first." He spun me to face him. "I don't like that the two of you have to go home at night." He furrowed his brow and studied my face, as if searching for a clue. "I want you to both move in with me. I mean, it doesn't have to be my place, but my house is bigger…"

A grin threatened to split my face. "You already asked Trevor, and he said yes?" I wasn't worried they'd talked about it without me, as long as they included me now.

"Not until you give me your answer." Evan said.

My smile grew wider. "He did say yes, or you wouldn't be asking me like this. And I'm saying yes, too."

Evan brushed his lips over mine, then cradled my face in his palms and deepened the kiss. I felt Trevor behind me, hand on my hip, breath on my neck. I gasped, still riding the rush of the moment, when Evan broke away.

"I didn't think you'd say no"—Evan gave me a sheepish smile—"but I was still a little worried."

"I'm definitely saying yes." I threw my arms around his neck. He squeezed me tight, Trevor's palm still on me.

I lingered in the shared embrace a little longer, savoring the moment and everything that led up to this point. We might hit a few bumps along the way, as our relationship grew and shifted, but we could work our way through any of it. Both of them—all three of us—we were a perfect discovery.

To meet Kathryn's best friend, Sydney, check out ROLL AGAINST BETRAYAL

www.ingramcontent.com/pod-product-compliance
Lightning Source LLC
LaVergne TN
LVHW091002080826
845145LV00003B/1103